The Banished Heart

A Novel

LIBI ASTAIRE

ASTER PRESS

First published 2012

Cover photo: iStockphoto.com/Claudio Divizia/alenavlad

ISBN: 978-0-9837931-7-5

Published and distributed by:

Aster Press
Kansas-Jerusalem
www.libiastaire.weebly.com

Watchman, what of the night?
Watchman, what of the night?

The watchman said:
Morning comes, and also the night.
If you will inquire, inquire.
Return, come.

— Isaiah 21:11-12

BERLIN

CHAPTER I

It is a dream. It is just a dream. Despite what the psychologists say – Freud and the others – I can explain it perfectly. It is just a bit of research, unimportant to the main argument of my thesis and therefore discarded, which, having nowhere else to go, has deposited itself in a crevice in my mind, like a seed blown by the wind to a place where a flower was never meant to grow. Even my recording it gives the dream an importance it would not have in other times.

Paul Hoffmann set down his pen. It *was* ridiculous that at five in the morning he was sitting at his desk and writing not the finishing touches to his thesis, but the details of this dream.

"Nerves," he muttered. But that was perfectly normal. Who wouldn't be nervous a few days before defending his thesis at the university? That's why this dream was such a bother. What he wanted most was a good night's sleep. Instead, every morning he was awoken at the same time, drenched in the same sweat, shaken with the same fear.

He therefore decided to write it down, that dream. Confront it in black on white, on good quality paper. Look at it in the light. Rob it of its mystery. Expose the bogey man for what it was – nothing – and make it disappear.

Disappear. Yes, that's what he'd do. He'd empty his mind of every last detail, pour it all out on the page, and then he would be free.

He picked up his pen, adjusted the lamp, and began to write:

The dream takes place in Spain. I know it is Spain, although I have never been to Spain, because I – no, not I – he is standing at the back of a square, in the shadows, grasping the hand of his young son. (I do not have a son. I am not married. So, of course, this person isn't me.)

The square is crowded with other people, families, with worried looks on their faces and small bundles in their hands. He slips away, with his son. They enter a place, a synagogue, I suppose. He points at something, a sort of light that hangs down low from the ceiling on a long brass chain. I cannot hear him speak, but – and this is the strange part – at that moment I am no longer "he" but the child. I follow his gaze. I see the flame, which is burning in a glass container. I hear him say something about eternal, or eternity. And then a rock comes crashing through the window. The container is shattered. Flames devour the room.

They push their way blindly through the smoke and fire, and emerge at a port. The place is swarming with people. They are among them – and they have been joined by the boy's mother – and they are being prodded forward by soldiers. Before them is the harbor, which is filled with an impossible number of ships, much too many to count. Some are still docked at the pier, while others have already departed, their ragged sails billowing in the wind, like phantom messengers from some woebegone isle.

The soldiers push them toward a gangway. But before they reach it, a group of soldiers march past and I – no, I mean the child – is pushed. His grip on his father's hand is severed. He is separated from his family. The child, being small, cannot see past the soldiers, who form a wall between him and his mother and father, who are being pushed up the gangway, onto the deck of the ship.

And still there are more people, a multitude of people, a dizzying swarm of Jews and soldiers and jeering crowds. The boy is pushed and shoved and turned and tumbled until, finally, there is a clearing in the crowd and he sees them – his father and his mother, who are standing on the deck of the ship.

"Papa! Mama!" he calls out.

The gangway is pulled up. The ship's sails are unfurled. And all the while the child is pushing his way to the edge of the dock. But when he reaches it, the ship has already sailed away.

"Mama!" he cries out. "Mama! Mama!"

This is when I awake, terrified, as though I were five years old and alone in the world, separated from my family and banished from my home, which is ridiculous, of course. This is not Spain in the year 1492, when the Jews were expelled from their country.

This is Germany, 1933.

He put down his pen a second time, dissatisfied. The details of the dream were there, but not the terror. He hadn't managed to convey that. It was as if the black ink upon the white paper was nothing more than a mask, a bloodless and superficial representation lacking the sublime fear that animated the dream. Perhaps the psychologists were right after all; perhaps there had been a time, when he was a small child, when he had gotten lost in a crowd, when he had experienced the fear of being abandoned, and now this memory and its accompanying terror were buried too deep in his psyche to be coaxed out by words. He must remember to ask his Grandmama Larissa.

The gauze curtain fluttered in the early morning breeze, and he realized that while he had been writing the night had ended. A pale light was streaming into his room, the small student apartment that he had rented, so that he would be more like the other students at the University of Berlin. Of course, by now everyone knew who he was, *that* Herr Hoffmann, heir to the Hoffmann fortune. But in the beginning he had wanted to blend in, choose his friends based upon their merits — just as he had hoped that he would be chosen based on his. And he had wanted to succeed in his studies based upon those same merits, not because his family could be relied upon to endow a chair or pay for a new building, or both, after he graduated.

First, though, he did have to graduate. He glanced over to the small plaster bust of William Shakespeare, which stood atop a typewritten manuscript — his thesis — whose pages gleamed ghostly white in the early morning light. The plaster bust was also white as death, as though it, too, were terrified of facing all the Herr Professors and students.

"Nerves," he muttered a second time. His thesis was sound; he knew it was. The topic had been suggested by his advisor, who had been generous with his time: "Shakespeare, the Slave Trade, and *The Merchant of Venice*: An Examination of William Shakespeare's Attitude toward the New World Order and the Breakdown of the Feudal Economic Model." No, there was no problem with that. Thus, there was absolutely no reason why he shouldn't graduate; the only real question was if he would graduate with honors, as he hoped.

"Mama! Mama!"

The paralysis. The cold sweat. The terror. It was back in an instant. But what fresh development was this? His dream had never before intruded upon his waking hours.

"Mama! Mama! Wake up! Mama!"

He realized that this was no dream. The voice was a real voice, and it was coming from the street below. He walked to the window and pulled aside the curtain. A small crowd had gathered around a woman who was lying in the street. Blood was trickling from the side of her head. Her sack of groceries had spilled its contents onto the ground — bread, eggs, milk. A young child, who was still wailing, knelt beside the woman.

Two men rushed outside from the building opposite; their faded black coats and unkempt beards marked them as Jews. They picked up the woman and carried her inside. The child followed. The crowd began to disperse. Then a man stepped from the shadows. He snatched up the loaf of bread from off the pavement and hurried away.

Paul let the curtain fall back into place.

ii.

The student café was already pulsating with talk and laughter when Meyer Aronstein pushed open the glass door. Not being an early riser himself, the morning scene at the café never failed to amaze him. How could it be that people were not only awake but vibrantly argumentative at such an hour?

"Meyer! Over here!"

He heard the familiar voice of his friend Franz Reese, and once the waiter blocking his view moved aside he saw the table where Franz and Joseph Wyler, another friend, were sitting.

"Good morning," he said, after he had shoved his way through the tangle of tables and chairs and sat down.

"You won't think so after you read this," said Joseph, pushing the morning newspaper in Meyer's direction.

Meyer inwardly groaned. He disliked discussing politics before he had had his breakfast. But Joseph was jabbing his finger at a headline, and Meyer knew he'd have no peace until the thing was read. "'New law to prevent overcrowding in German schools and universities,'" he read aloud. "Another law. How industrious they are." He pushed the newspaper aside, preferring to concentrate, instead, on the roll and coffee that the waiter had flung on the table. "Why is there never any sugar?" he asked, to no one, really, since the waiter had already dashed off to another table.

Joseph snatched back the paper. "Hitler's only been in power for four months and he's already ..."

"There's Paul," said Franz. "Paul! Over here!"

Joseph didn't wait for Paul Hoffmann to sit down to continue with his speech. He didn't need an attentive audience; any batch of bodies grouped near enough to hear would do. "Like I was saying, Hitler's only been in power since January—Morning, Paul—and he's already convinced the country to limit Jewish enrollment to just 1.5 percent of the university student population. Do you know what that means?"

Paul had no trouble catching the eye of the waiter, who knew to expect a generous tip if he was quick about bringing Paul's coffee. "It means you'd better pass your exams this time, Joseph, because you're not going to get a third chance."

"This isn't a joke," said Franz. "My brother is supposed to be starting university in the fall, and he still hasn't gotten his letter of acceptance."

"You see?" said Joseph.

Paul, who had received two sugar cubes with his coffee, passed one over to Meyer. "Joseph, don't be such a prophet of doom," he said, watching the tiny white crystals dissolve into the bitter brew. "Any day now the German people will wake up and realize that this whole nonsense of boycotting Jewish businesses and firing Jewish professionals is, well, nonsense. Then there will be new elections and Hitler and his gang will be sent packing."

When no one said anything, Paul turned to Meyer, whom he considered to be his best friend at the university, and said, "You at least agree with me, don't you?"

"My father got his dismissal notice yesterday."

Joseph let out a low whistle. "Because of the new Civil Service law?"

Meyer nodded.

"I'm sorry," said Paul, with less emotion than he actually felt. Hearing about another person's misfortune always made him feel uncomfortable.

"It's easy for you to be optimistic about the future, Paul. You're rich," said Franz, whose family was just barely middle class. "If things get worse, you can leave Germany whenever you like."

"And go wherever you like," added Joseph, whose parents had come to Germany as penniless refugees from Poland after World War I and still hadn't established themselves financially.

"Not me. I could never leave Germany," said Paul. "I'm too German. When I was five years old my parents took me on a vacation to the Italian Riviera and I was sick the entire time."

"That's no proof," said Joseph. "If I were surrounded by rich people all day, I'd be sick too."

"Communist."

"Socialist. There's a difference, and you know it."

"Come on, you two," said Franz. "We're not interested in hearing that old argument again."

Meyer, who had been silently eyeing Paul during the conversation, didn't know if he should speak or not. Sometimes he admired his friend's superb self-possession, which he knew was one of the many gifts that came with possessing great wealth. Other times, and this was one of those times, he wondered if that wealth didn't blind a person to the true state of things; the gold glittered, but the golden casket was empty, if he correctly recalled Shakespeare's play. Since a silence in the conversation had ensued, he decided to hazard offending his friend and said, "What if the faculty doesn't accept your thesis, Paul? You won't graduate. What will happen to your plans then?"

"That's right," said Franz. "If your thesis isn't accepted, you can say goodbye to your career as Herr Doktor Professor of Literature."

"Why shouldn't the faculty accept it?" Paul rolled his eyes to emphasize his contempt for the notion. It was one thing for him to have doubts at five in the morning in the privacy of his room, and quite another for someone like Franz Reese to express those same doubts in a public place like the student café. In truth, he was irritated with Meyer, as well, but decided to let his comment pass; Meyer's usually clear vision was probably clouded this morning by the bad news concerning his father. To his chagrin, though, Meyer was continuing to badger him.

"Isn't your thesis about how Shakespeare originally wrote *The Merchant of Venice* to defend a Jew and stop him from being hanged?"

"Dr. Lopez was a Converso. He was born a Portuguese Jew, but by the time Shakespeare knew him he had become an English Protestant."

"I bet the Elizabethans cared about that as much as the Nazis do," said Joseph.

Paul again rolled his eyes, this time at Joseph. "And what do you know about the Elizabethans, Herr Wyler? I thought your knowledge of English history and literature begins and ends with Karl Marx."

"Who cares about the Elizabethans, or Marx," said Franz, whose expression was growing gloomier by the minute. "It's the German Students' Association we have to worry about. They've been putting up posters all over the university. They could make trouble for you."

"That gaggle of over-zealous freshmen? What have I to do with them, or they with me?"

"You don't have to do anything, Paul," replied Franz. "Being Jewish is enough to set them off."

"It's all just talk. No one with an ounce of sense takes them seriously."

Now it was Joseph's turn to roll his eyes, and he did it with relish. "You may think they're a joke, but that's only because you don't know the first thing about Jewish history."

"Someday when I have more time you must enlighten me."

"I can do it right now, and in one sentence: When the *goyim* say they want to get rid of the Jews, you can believe them."

There was an uneasy pause, and then Paul, noticing that the café was starting to empty since the first class of the morning would begin shortly, rose from the table and said, "My friends, I appreciate your concern about my future, but you needn't worry. The Department of Literature at the University of Berlin is as high above the petty doings of the street as William Shakespeare is above Joseph Goebbels and his Nazi propaganda machine. And besides, I did change the topic of my thesis."

CHAPTER II

Herr Doktor Professor Thomas Hurst, a senior professor of literature at the University of Berlin, possessed what he considered to be a singular blessing: the ability to focus on only that which he wished to perceive and blissfully ignore all the rest.

The quality was useful for a scholar, of course, since the ability to concentrate on a difficult text, without becoming distracted by the flurry of extraneous thoughts that attacked many the moment they settled into their chair at the university library, made the research and writing much easier. But, and he wouldn't necessarily admit this to any but his closest colleagues, the real value of that dogged concentration came when he had to traverse the labyrinth of corridors that led from the lecture room to his office. It wasn't that he disliked his students, but he did dislike the mock-respectful salutations of those who mistakenly believed they were original thinkers destined for academic greatness as much as he abhorred the cringing greetings of those who rightfully worried about a future of failure. He therefore found it convenient to cloak himself within an air of what some might construe as absent-mindedness but what he liked to think of as occupying a higher realm.

As he strode down the corridor, lecture notes in hand, he therefore hoped that the two students with their noses in a poster stuck onto the wall would keep them there. But no, they looked up at the sound of his footsteps, which seemed to echo noisily in the hall.

"Good morning, Herr Doktor Professor Hurst," they said with mock-respect.

"Good morning," he replied, nodding his head in their direction. His eye caught a glimpse of the poster that the two had been reading with such interest. It was one of the posters put up by the German Students' Association. He quickly looked away and continued down the corridor. Behind him, he could hear the two students whisper something and then laugh.

For a moment, he wondered if he should stop and say something. This laughter—laughter out loud—was something new, something that had started with the present term. It was one thing for students to make fun of their professors in the beer halls and cafés and in their rooms; that was as much a part of student life as getting drunk and discussing the world's problems until dawn. But in his day, a student would never laugh at a professor while he was in the professor's presence, not even at a junior professor, not even to the professor's back.

Yes, he really should turn around and say something. But then again, perhaps he was being too sensitive; perhaps it wasn't him they were laughing at, after all. If that were the case, he'd only make a fool of himself, if he reprimanded the students over nothing—and give some people yet another excuse to call for his retirement.

Absent-minded Hurst is getting more senile by the day, I hear. They say he's been accusing the students of imaginary insults. It's about time he stepped aside and let some fresh blood into the department, don't you think?

No, he'd better not risk it. He therefore continued on toward his office, but to his chagrin the very person whom he wished to avoid above all others—Herr Doktor Professor Laufer, the new chairman of the department—sprang out of his office and blocked Professor Hurst's path. Unlike the students, Professor Hurst could hardly pretend to ignore the chairman. He therefore braced himself for whatever new pronouncement was coming—for Herr Doktor Professor Laufer always seemed to have an endless supply of pronouncements.

~ 14 ~

"Hurst, you've saved me a memorandum," said Professor Laufer, with his usual jovial manner that signified nothing.

"Yes, Herr Doktor Professor?" Professor Hurst would never dream of addressing a fellow professor by only his last name, omitting his title, not even a professor who was several decades younger, like Professor Laufer.

"Faculty meeting tomorrow. Two o'clock."

"May I ask the topic of this meeting?"

"Changes in the curriculum. I expect all the senior members of the faculty to be there. "

"For our input?"

"Germany is moving forward, Professor Hurst. She'll get there much quicker if we all march together."

Although Professor Hurst wasn't sure about where Germany was headed, he certainly had no objection to seeing his department chairman march quickly down the hall, especially since his own path lay in the opposite direction. Yet once again he was prevented from reaching the calm oasis of his office. Professor Shultz, a junior professor in his department, was lying in wait for him.

"Herr Doktor Professor Hurst, could I please have a word with you?"

"Yes, but only a word, Professor Shultz. I have a meeting with a student."

"It's about those posters. They've sprung up everywhere during the last few days. Have you read what they say?"

The young man pointed to the wall, which had been recently adorned by one of the placards. Professor Hurst adjusted his eyeglasses and read:

STUDENTS!
AN UN-GERMAN SPIRIT
HAS CORRUPTED OUR UNIVERSITY!
CLEANSE THE UNIVERSITY OF BERLIN OF
NON-ARYAN INFLUENCES!
GERMAN STUDENTS' ASSOCIATION

When the senior professor was silent, Professor Shultz said, "I thought, if the faculty, or at least some members in our department, were to organize a meeting ... to discuss ... it might ..."

"I must go," said Professor Hurst, glancing at his watch.

He hurried down the corridor, wrapping himself even more tightly in his "higher realm," determined that nothing more should intrude upon his progress.

Professor Shultz watched, his eyes blinking quickly, as they often did when his mind was agitated. Then he reached for the poster and ripped it from the wall.

Professor Hurst, who had heard the noise, stopped and turned. He saw the young man crumple the poster in his hands.

"Come to my office at 11:25. We'll discuss the matter then."

"Thank you, Herr Doktor Professor!"

ii.

To Professor Hurst's great relief, he reached his office without further incident. He nodded briefly to his secretary and to the young man sitting in the anteroom, who had sprung to his feet. "I'll be with you in a moment, Herr Hoffmann."

"Thank you, Herr Doktor Professor," Paul replied.

Professor Hurst quickly closed the door to his inner office behind him. He still had a few minutes before the scheduled appointment with the student, a few minutes to call his own. He put his lecture notes on his desk, and then went to open the window. He liked to have plenty of fresh air in his office, especially during the hours when he had to see his students. Perhaps it was a vain hope that the fresh air would stimulate fresh ideas, but it was a certainty that a stuffy room would send them all to sleep.

For a moment he allowed himself the luxury of looking outside and contemplating the view of the university grounds, which never disappointed. The university buildings stood solidly on their foundations, grand, even monumental, a fitting tribute to the lofty ideals of excellence in scholarship, dedication to truth, belief in the progress of man. These were the ideals that had animated his life for more than six decades. They were ideals that he had tried to pass on to his students, year after year, class after class.

But even while he was thinking those lofty thoughts, he couldn't help but notice the scene that was taking place below, in the square, a scene that had become so typical during the past few months. One of the Jewish students crossing the square was "accidently" tripped by a German student. When the Jewish young man fell, the crowd, which had quickly gathered, laughed. Yes, the University of Berlin was a jovial place these days, Professor Hurst thought grimly as he turned away from the window, a place full of mean-spirited laughter and fun.

He sat down at his desk and reached for Paul Hoffmann's thesis, which was sitting in a pile with several others. As he thumbed through the pages, he frowned. This was going to be an unpleasant meeting. Better to get it over with, then.

He went back to the door and opened it. "Herr Hoffmann? Please, come in." When he had returned to his desk, he motioned to the chair opposite and said, "Sit down. Sit down."

"Thank you, Herr Doktor Professor," said Paul, sitting in the chair with his back straight, so that he would not give the appearance of seeming too casually comfortable in the presence of the senior professor. He knew that Professor Hurst considered such details to be important.

"Herr Hoffmann, this thesis of yours on *The Merchant of Venice*, would you say that it follows the outline we developed at the beginning of the academic year?"

"There are a few changes."

"A few? I assure you, I have given this manuscript a most careful reading, yet I fail to see what it has to do with the original topic, which was, if I recall ..."

Professor Hurst fumbled through the files sitting on his desk, until he found Paul Hoffmann's folder, which had become unattached from the thesis manuscript. Then he rummaged some more, while he searched for the page with the outline of the thesis. Paul watched in what he hoped conveyed a respectful silence. He liked Professor Hurst, even if the man was a bit over the hill and rambled during his lectures. Somehow the senior professor always managed to insert at least one startling original insight into Shakespeare's text, which made attending the lecture worthwhile.

"Here we are," said Professor Hurst, finding at last the page he had been looking for. "'Shakespeare and *The Banished Heart*: A Re-examination of *The Merchant of Venice* in Light of New Findings Regarding William Shakespeare's Relationship with Dr. Rodrigo Lopez and London's Converso Community.'"

"I know you felt strongly about the original topic, but Herr Doktor Professor Laufer felt otherwise," Paul replied.

"Professor Laufer? I was under the impression that I am your faculty advisor."

"Professor Laufer informed me that he would be my advisor after he was appointed the new chairman of the department in March. There should be a memorandum in my file. I was told you would be informed."

"I see." For a moment, Professor Hurst doubted himself. Perhaps he had been notified, and he had forgotten. No. He was certain that there would be no memorandum, if he were to look for one. It was yet another insult. But these internal quarrels were not the fault of the student sitting opposite him, and so he said, struggling to remain in control of his voice, "And Professor Laufer suggested you change the topic of your thesis?"

"Yes, he thought the original topic — with its discussion of Shakespeare's involvement in the Lopez affair — wasn't appropriate, in view of the times."

"The times?"

"Yes, so he advised me to change the topic to one that would be less controversial."

"Please excuse my ignorance, Herr Hoffmann, which appears to be vaster than I had previously imagined, but I thought the search for truth was above 'the times.'"

"Your reputation is secure, Herr Doktor Professor. Mine is not."

"Meaning?"

"I want to graduate."

"I see. So in your opinion, as a Jew, do you ..."

"Excuse me, Herr Doktor Professor, but I do nothing as a Jew. I am a German."

"Very well, as a German, is it then your opinion that there is no place in a German university for defending a controversial viewpoint? Should the truth be abandoned if it could prove to be detrimental to one's career?"

Paul glanced toward the open window, wishing it offered some practical means of escape. It wouldn't do to antagonize Professor Hurst since he was sure to be on the committee that would decide whether or not to accept his thesis. But it wasn't his fault that no one had informed Professor Hurst about the change in his thesis advisor, and he resented being the punching bag for the professor's bruised ego. He therefore said, still maintaining a respectful tone, "I was only following Professor Laufer's instructions, Herr Doktor Professor. No offence was intended."

"I see. And what happened to the manuscript I gave you? Since you have no use for it, is there a reason why you haven't yet returned it?"

The question shouldn't have caught Paul unprepared, but it did. He remembered his conversation with Professor Laufer quite clearly. Professor Laufer had been surprisingly insistent that Paul give him the manuscript, which was called

The Banished Heart and supposedly had been written in the early 1600s by a Jewish eye-witness to the Lopez affair, Henry Rivers, a Converso who later had escaped to Constantinople and returned to his Jewish faith.

"Professor Laufer expressed an interest in seeing the manuscript," said Paul, feeling his cheeks grow warm, "and so I gave it to him."

Professor Hurst opened his mouth, but words failed to come out. When he had regained sufficient control of his emotions, he asked, "Did Professor Laufer say why he was interested in the manuscript?"

Behind the calm mask on his face, Paul inwardly groaned. He detested these petty departmental intrigues, and he wished that the elderly professor would leave him out of them. For the first time he felt that he was seeing Professor Hurst as he really was—an old man well past his prime who was making one last desperate attempt at lasting fame. Even the office, which Paul had once thought was charmingly romantic, furnished as it was with its solid wood cupboards and over-stuffed chairs, now seemed only pathetically nineteenth century; the office, like the man who occupied it, was a relic from a previous age which was rightly about to be swept away.

"Did Professor Laufer perhaps say that he suspected it was a forgery?" asked Professor Hurst, his voice rising too high, despite his efforts to control the pitch.

"I believe there is always that possibility with these old manuscripts that suddenly turn up." Paul then added, to soften the blow, "It happens in art, as well, when a supposedly new work by an Old Master is discovered."

"But this was not a new work by Shakespeare. It was a personal history written by a man who claimed to have been a friend of both the playwright and Dr. Lopez. And it was found in our own university, lodged in a small storage room with other seemingly unimportant manuscripts from the period, where it had been gathering dust for centuries."

"Yes, I know that's what you said. But Professor Laufer did mention, in passing, you understand – and, of course, it all does sound rather like a cheap thriller – but in his opinion, anyone who had free access to the university's library and archives could have put the document in that room and covered it with dust so that it looked like it had been there for quite some time."

"And what do you think, Herr Hoffmann? Is the manuscript a forgery or a faithful witness?"

"I only had time to read it through once."

"But surely it made an impression upon you, as a ... student of Shakespeare. When we know so little about the man Shakespeare, surely any new information that comes to light must arouse interest. Even after only one reading, you must have formed some sort of an opinion."

"To be honest, I found the claims disturbing."

"Because?"

"For one thing, who is this Henry Rivers? He's the one who says that Shakespeare was part of the Earl of Essex's spy network, at the time that *Merchant* was written, but what do we know about Rivers, other than what he says about himself in the manuscript? How do we know that he is a reliable witness?"

"True, he is only an unknown, faceless Jew. But what do we know about Shakespeare?"

"We have his plays."

"Exactly. Your thesis was supposed to examine the merits of Rivers's argument in light of the text of *The Merchant of Venice* – the text's inconsistencies regarding Shylock, and so forth."

When Paul was silent, Professor Hurst continued, "Herr Hoffmann, the thesis topic I suggested would have given you more than an opportunity to graduate. It would have given you an opportunity to make your mark in the international field of Shakespearian scholarship. It would have given you an opportunity to delve into the problem of why Shakespeare – who showed such generosity of spirit to so many different types of people — was so harsh, so mean-spirited, when it came to the Jew, to Shylock. For the life of me, I do not understand why you did not come to me when Professor Laufer asked you to change the topic. I might have been able to reason with him."

"I don't think you would have succeeded, Professor Hurst. Professor Laufer was very insistent that the manuscript, even if it is authentic, should be suppressed."

"Suppressed? You are aware, Herr Hoffmann, that the manuscript I gave you was an original copy. I doubt there is another copy of it anywhere in the world. Why did you give it to him? What right ..."

Professor Hurst was again aware that he was losing control, and it would not do to have a fit of rage in front of a student. For all he knew, Paul Hoffmann might be one of Laufer's spies. If he lost control, ranted and raged about Laufer's audacity, his over-stepping of bounds, his ignorance about the way a university department should be run and research conducted — if he did all that before a student who was clearly part of Laufer's inner circle, all he would achieve would be the handing over of another piece of evidence for why the university should ask him to retire.

But would that be so terrible, he wondered, as he listened to what the student sitting across from him was saying.

"Sometimes the truth needs to be sacrificed, Professor Hurst, for the higher good."

"I see." Professor Hurst took a last look at the thesis outline, which he was still holding in his hand, before tossing the page into a nearby waste bin. "Thank you, Herr Hoffmann. This conversation has been most enlightening. That will be all."

Moments after Paul left the room, there was a knock on the door and Professor Shultz entered.

"Excuse me, Herr Doktor Professor, but about that matter we were discussing, the posters."

"Yes, Professor Shultz, I've thought it over. There is no reason for me to get involved."

CHAPTER III

Although Paul tried to dismiss the distasteful interview with Professor Hurst from his thoughts, he found that it lingered. He therefore asked Meyer to join him in an excursion to a nearby stationery store, which was one of his favorite places in Berlin.

He didn't talk about it much, feeling that an artist should be praised by others and not promote himself, but Paul considered himself to be first and foremost a poet. Like many young poets, he found it easier to dream about writing the perfect sonnet than to actually write one. Therefore, his frequent trips to the stationery store, where he would peruse the inks and pens and lovingly finger the different samples of high-quality writing paper — weighing each one in his hand to gauge its feel of importance — gave him the illusion of belonging to the brotherhood of poets while he waited for inspiration, and its companions fame and fortune, to find him.

Meyer had agreed to join him. But Paul was not so immersed in his study of the new samples of writing paper that had arrived since his last visit to not notice that his friend's thoughts were many miles away. "Did your father at least get any severance pay?" he asked, correctly guessing that the dismissal of Herr Aronstein from the Civil Service was still foremost in Meyer's mind.

"No."

"If your family needs any help ..."

"Thanks, but we'll manage."

Once again, Paul had the uneasy feeling of being placed in a situation over which he had no control and which offered no escape. It wasn't his fault that some people were rich and basked in the sunny, warming rays of good fortune, while some were poor and chased by the dark clouds of trouble and woe. It was true that the practical problems of the world didn't weigh heavily on his mind, as they seemed to do with Joseph, and so some might think him callous. But he had the heart and soul of a poet and surely that excused much. And he liked to think that he genuinely cared about his friends, which was why he felt hurt when he did try to help and his efforts were coldly rebuffed.

He set down the piece of stationery he had been examining and picked up another, which was much less expensive. "You shouldn't think that my family is entirely unaffected by what's happening in the country. There have been some incidents at my father's factories."

"What happened?"

"Some equipment was smashed. A few slogans were scrawled on the walls, that sort of thing." He was grateful that Meyer didn't ask for more details, since he didn't know much more. His Grandmama Larissa, his father's widowed mother, who ruled unchallenged over the family mansion near the Opernplatz, didn't like to discuss unpleasant things and so the topic had been dropped as rapidly as it had been brought up at the Sunday dinner table.

"This one seems to have a nice weight to it," said Meyer, selecting yet another piece of stationery.

"Do you think so? With so many choices, it's hard to decide."

The Jewish store owner, who had been following the conversation from behind the counter, decided that it was time to offer his professional advice. "If I may offer my opinion, the paper you are holding, Herr Hoffmann, is very good for writing business letters—letters that are written quickly on a typewriter and just as quickly thrown away."

"And that one?" Paul asked, pointing to the paper that Meyer was holding.

"That one is for the ages. Like good poetry, its charms will neither wither nor fade."

"You've just said the magic word," said Meyer. "Herr Hoffmann is a poet."

"I suspected as much," said the store owner, who had suspected no such thing until that moment, but didn't mind humoring rich young men who had money to spend on expensive stationery and fancy pens.

"I am a poet only to my friends," Paul rather weakly protested. "The German Society of Poetry has a different opinion entirely."

"He's being too modest," Meyer said to the store owner, who nodded his head sympathetically, even while he wondered how much longer it would take until the gentleman made his selection. His lunch was announcing itself by the aroma wafting through the back door that led to his family's apartment, and his stomach was starting to rumble. But still Herr Hoffmann's friend was talking, and so the shop owner pretended to listen with interest.

"Herr Hoffmann has already had his poems published in several ..."

The sound of broken glass crashing to the floor made them all look in the direction of what had been just a moment before the store's front window. At the same time, the wife of the store owner rushed into the room. She was about to say something, but her husband silently motioned to the two young men and said, "Don't worry, my dear, everyone is fine."

She glanced from the young men to the rock sitting in the middle of the shattered glass. "I'll have this cleaned up in a moment," she said to Paul and Meyer. "We apologize for the disturbance."

While his wife went to find a broom, the store owner said to Paul, "Shall I wrap up a box of this stationery for you, Herr Hoffmann?"

Paul took another look at the destroyed window and said, "I'll take ten boxes. Please deliver them to my rooms."

When they had returned to the street, Meyer couldn't resist commenting, "Ten boxes of stationery? Are you intending to write an opus?"

"Do you think the money will cover the price of a new window?"

"I should think so, since each piece of that stationery seems to be worth its weight in gold."

Paul was about to say something in reply, but Meyer stopped him. "Listen. Look invisible."

"What?"

"Parade passing by."

By this time Paul could also hear the music. Without saying another word, the two stepped into the shadows of a recessed doorway and waited.

The music grew louder as a troop of Brown Shirts turned into the street. At the head of the procession were drummers who beat out the tempo of a rousing march, while the players of the brass instruments behind them blasted out the melody. A few of the marchers carried flags that bore the Nazi insignia, and the fluttering of their flags was answered by crowds of people who had appeared on the balconies overlooking the street and were waving their handkerchiefs, some in time to the spirited music. A crowd had also gathered below and they danced beside the goose-stepping men, cheering them on.

It only took a few minutes for the troop to pass through the street and turn down another, but it seemed like an eternity to Paul and Meyer, who hoped they wouldn't be noticed in their hiding place, which only partially concealed their presence. When at last the show was over and the crowd dispersed, they stepped back into the light and resumed their stroll down the street.

"Is it me that's crazy, or Berlin?" asked Meyer.

"Let's hope it's you. One can't put an entire city on the couch."

"Maybe it's time we tried."

"The problem, of course, is that there aren't enough decent jobs. If the unemployed could channel their energy into earning an honest paycheck, they would lose their taste for parading around in those ridiculous costumes."

"Paul, those Brown Shirts are thugs. They enjoy dressing up in uniforms and beating up innocent people."

"That's because they're the ones who have been hit the hardest by the previous government's misguided social and economic policies. It's no wonder that they feel angry and frustrated."

Meyer stared at his friend. They rarely discussed politics, preferring instead to untangle knotty philosophical problems or debate the virtues of recent books and plays. He therefore wondered whose views Paul was expressing, his own or someone else's, as he asked, "Are you making excuses for them?"

"Facts are facts. Take your intended profession, for example."

"What about it?"

"Jews make up less than one percent of the German population, and yet twenty-five percent of the medical students are Jewish. Twenty-five percent! And the same is true with the legal profession. I had a hard time believing it, until Professor Laufer, my department head, showed me the statistics. It's all there in black and white."

Meyer had heard some disquieting rumors about Paul's department chairman, but he had never discussed them with his friend. The truth was that during the last few weeks they hadn't seen as much of each other as usual; Paul had been busy making the final revisions to his thesis, while he had his own examinations to worry about. He was surprised to hear Paul mouthing the same propaganda that one read in the newspapers, but he supposed that each person had to find his own way of coping with the changing events, which were changing at a confusing, dizzy speed. But there were limits, even for Jews like them, who considered themselves to be Jews in name only. When Jewish professionals were being attacked, Meyer felt he couldn't let the matter pass without protest. He therefore said, "If we're good doctors and lawyers, what does it matter how many of us there are?"

"It matters because this Jewish domination of all the top professions causes ill will."

"So you agree with the new law limiting university enrollment?"

"Hitler's solutions may be extreme ..."

"Thank you, for at least admitting that."

"But we have to understand the pain of the German people. They feel like their country has been stolen away from them. And in a way it has."

"So what's your solution, Paul? Move to Palestine with Joseph and become a farmer?"

"Don't be ridiculous."

Meyer was on the verge of stating what he felt was obvious, that Professor Laufer had neglected to mention another group that aroused the wrath of the German people, namely fabulously wealthy Jewish industrialists, but he didn't. He was once again reminded of the vast expanse that separated him from his friend. While Paul's great wealth would always enable him to hide in his ivory tower—and even build one of his own should a German university not be willing to provide one for his use—he, Meyer, had no such assurance to fall back upon. If the government started limiting the number of Jewish doctors who could practice their profession, where would that leave him? Cleaning streets?

Paul, for his part, was annoyed not so much with his friend, but with life in general. There seemed to be some dark cloud hovering over the day, coating every event, whether large or small, with an acrid taste. One couldn't even take a stroll on a beautiful spring afternoon without having the politics of the day poison the air. And although he didn't like to admit it, those politics had also sullied the air of his beloved Department of Literature. It was all the fault of Professor Hurst, too. Paul had wanted to write his thesis about Hamlet, that tragic, poetic figure. It was Hurst who insisted that he write about *The Merchant of Venice*, instead, a play for which he felt no connection, no sympathy. He had pretended to be enthusiastic about the topic Hurst had suggested and about the research, but what did he care, really, about the political machinations of the Elizabethan period? He cared about poetry, lofty expressions of the soul, the idea of the "pathetic" and the "sublime," as set down by that great German poet and playwright Friedrich Schiller. That's what he had wanted to write about—Schiller's concept of tragic art and how it applied to *Hamlet*. To apply such concepts to Shylock and *The Merchant of Venice* had seemed like a joke in the poorest taste. And then things had gone from bad to worse when Laufer was appointed head of the department and told him to change his thesis topic. It was no longer politics that was his subject but economics— and not just any economics, but the dirty, distasteful economics of the slave trade and moneylending and what on earth did his soul have to do with all that?

He would have liked to roar the question, which seemed to grab his entire body with an intense force now that he had allowed it to find expression, but of course he didn't. For one thing, a person didn't roar like a madman on a Berlin street. For another, he was momentarily shocked into paralysis. There, standing on the sidewalk, a few feet ahead, was his nemesis, his enemy, his foe who had soured his waking hours during the past several weeks—Shylock, himself— who was defiantly staring Paul in the face.

It wasn't a real Shylock, of course. Paul and Meyer had reached a kiosk and stuck onto the thing, in a prominent place, was a hideous black and white theatre poster for a production of *The Merchant of Venice*. The obscenely grotesque depiction of Shylock drooling over his drawn knife made Paul feel ill. Yet he couldn't look away. It was as if he was looking into some terrifying fairy-tale mirror that trapped the soul of whoever looked into it, rooting the person to the spot, preventing him from escaping from its grasp.

Meyer also saw the poster, but for him it cast no spell. "Let's go," he said.

"Where? How do we ever get away from that?" Paul gestured in the direction of the poster.

"You can't let the Nazis define who you are. If you start believing you're a Shylock, and a cartoon Shylock at that, you'll go mad."

"So who am I? The world calls me a Jew, and yet I don't identify with anything Jewish. So what does it mean when the world points its angry finger at me and says, 'Jew!'?"

"Religion isn't my strong point."

"So explain it to me as a doctor. When you examine samples of Jewish blood and Christian blood under the microscope, what exactly do you see? Is it so obvious that the possessor of Jewish blood should be hated and despised by humanity, while the other man is honored and accepted?"

"A person is more than flesh and blood. There is also the soul."

"Ah, the soul. 'A wretched soul, bruised with adversity. An ill-favored thing, sir, but mine own.'"

"Shakespeare?"

"Mangled Shakespeare."

"Like that Shylock," said Meyer, nodding toward the poster. "It's a pity your Shakespeare wrote that play. I haven't read your thesis, but it seems to me that if his intent was to defend the Jews he failed rather miserably. "

"It wasn't his fault."

"I suppose it was the fault of that Jewish doctor, Rodriguez or Lopez or whatever his name was."

Before Paul could reply, Meyer spotted his streetcar and, with a wave of goodbye, dashed off to catch it. "See you tomorrow," Meyer called out from the step, before disappearing inside the car.

Paul waved in reply and then returned his gaze to the poster, still fascinated by the pale, leering face framed by greasy long hair and straggly beard, the claw-like hand that grasped the hilt of the dagger, the almost reptilian quality of the figure that was part nightmare and part beast. Was that what people saw when they saw him, he wondered, as the acrid taste again filled his mouth. Why, when he saw himself as a sublime Hamlet contemplating the mortality of poor Yorick, had he been thrust onto some crazy world stage where he was being forced to contemplate the degraded Jewishness of despised Shylock, instead?

CHAPTER IV

Paul might have temporarily exchanged his opulent home near the Opernplatz for more modest student quarters, but he wasn't prepared to give up every luxury. One of those luxuries, which he really considered to be a necessity, was a wireless, so that he could listen to the classical music programs on the radio. His landlady, Frau Koch, had gaped in amazement when the console was delivered, even before she knew what it was. When the cabinet doors were closed, the wireless looked like any other piece of beautiful mahogany furniture—and that was enough to set it apart from the other furnishings in the boarding house, which were comfortable but hardly first class. However, when he had opened the center doors and revealed the large horn speaker sitting inside, Frau Koch was speechless. And after he fiddled with the knobs sitting on top of the cabinet and the music began to play, she stared and stared into the dark recesses of the speaker as though she expected the orchestra to come marching out of it at any minute.

Of course, after a while Frau Koch became used to the contraption, and Paul suspected that sometimes, when he was at the university and she was cleaning his room, she turned the machine on and listened to the programs. He didn't mind. Classical music was a love that he was happy to share.

But on this particular day Paul was more than usually grateful for his wireless. It wasn't just that the music soothed his rattled nerves, but it gave him something else to think about; for the day had finally arrived. In a short while he would be standing in the lecture hall and defending his thesis.

He was scrutinizing his appearance in the mirror—his tailor had done an excellent job with the new suit, he decided—when the classical music program ended and a news program came on. He barely lent an ear to the opening advertisement, but when the program switched to its main story Paul walked over to the radio cabinet and turned up the volume.

"*Last night, students from the University of Cologne staged a massive book-burning ceremony in the university's main square,*" the radio announcer was saying. "*This morning we have with us in the studio the national president of the German Students' Association, Herr Kurt Ellersiek. Good morning, Herr Ellersiek.*"

"*Good morning,*" said another voice, that of the Association's national president.

"*Can you tell us what happened in Cologne last night?*"

"*It was a beautiful night; one that should make all Germans proud.*"

Paul would have continued to listen, but there was a knock at the door. It was Frau Koch, whose face was beaming as if he were her own son.

"It's today, isn't it? Today is the day you'll be defending your thesis?"

"Yes, it is."

"I wish you good luck, Herr Hoffmann."

"Thank you, Frau Koch."

Frau Koch was about to go, when she realized that she was still holding an envelope in her hand. "I almost forgot. Here's a telegram for you. From your mother and father, I expect."

"I expect so," he said, accepting the telegram. "Thank you."

When she had gone, he opened the telegram and read:

Dearest Paul,
Good luck today. We know you will make us proud.

He put down the telegram and returned to the mirror, to adjust his tie. Meanwhile, the radio interview was continuing.

"*How many books would you say the students burned, Herr Ellersiek?*"

"*I can't give an exact number, but they made a lovely bonfire.*"

"*And by the time a new day dawned, the University of Cologne was cleansed of all books written by Jewish authors?*"

"*That is correct. And I challenge the students in Heidelberg, Berlin, and universities throughout Germany to ...*"

Paul fiddled with the dials, trying to find a different radio station, a place in the airwaves where beautiful music was playing. When his search was rewarded with static, he switched off the machine.

ii.

It was an achingly beautiful day and as Paul walked toward the University of Berlin, with his thesis securely stored in his leather attaché case, he pitied all the workers who were seated at their desks, entombed inside the great brick buildings. Since he was early, he decided to treat himself to a coffee at an outdoor café on the Unter den Linden. Although the linden trees lining the famous boulevard were only just beginning to blossom, the sky was a brilliant blue and the sun was warm against his face.

He removed a copy of Schiller's poems from his briefcase and as he read and sipped his coffee, which was strong and sweet, he could almost convince himself that no matter what happened during the next few hours, it wouldn't matter. As long as there were cafés and poetry and birds singing in the trees—not to mention gold-trimmed pens and beautiful writing paper—life was worth living. For several glorious moments he felt part of that sublime entity known as the universe; his smallness didn't bother him, because he was connected to something so much greater. Just by virtue of being alive he could claim a place in that magnificent struggle for meaning and futurity, and all the people who had ever lived and loved and dreamed and strived, they were his brothers, his friends.

But then the coffee cup was empty and a mass of gray clouds moved in, obscuring the sun and depositing a chill upon the place. He paid and continued down the boulevard. When he neared the university he was only partially surprised to see that Meyer was waiting for him. No one knew better than Meyer that despite his outward nonchalant appearance, Paul needed a dose of support and encouragement. But he was surprised to see that Meyer's sister Sarah had accompanied her brother; he and Sarah had rubbed each other the wrong way on their first meeting and their friendship, if one could call it that, had never improved.

When Sarah took one of Paul's arms and tried to turn him around, he was therefore irritated and wondered what obnoxious prank the girl intended to play on him this time. "Meyer, tell your sister to let go of me," he protested, while he tried to shake off her grasp.

"We're doing this for your own good," said Sarah, forcibly dragging Paul away from the university square.

"You're ruining my new suit, that's what you're doing."

"Never mind about your suit, Paul," said Meyer.

"There's going to be trouble today," Sarah added.

"What sort of trouble?" Paul had stopped struggling.

"The German Students' Association is organizing it," said Meyer. "All of the Jewish students are being warned to go home."

"Paul, why don't you treat us to the movies?" said Sarah. "Surely what's happening at the University of Berlin can't be the only comedy playing in town."

Paul regarded the pair for several moments. He knew that Meyer wasn't one to get excited at every little thing. If anything, Sarah was even tougher than her older brother. But today he was going to be stronger than the two of them put together. "You two can do what you like," he said, tightening his grip upon the leather handle of his attaché case with one hand, while straightening his tie with the other. "I'm not going to let a few pyromaniacs chase me away."

He turned away from them, ready to stride forward with purpose-filled steps, but his path was immediately blocked by the approach of Franz and Joseph, who were apparently coming from the university.

"You heard?" said Joseph.

"We heard," Sarah replied. "But Paul insists on marching into the lion's den."

"Why?" asked Franz.

"Sir Galahad has to defend his thesis."

"Don't be a fool, Paul," said Joseph.

"He's right," said Meyer, still hoping he could convince his friend. "Your professors will surely understand."

"They have to," said Franz. "If there's going to be a big Nazi demonstration ..."

"It won't happen in the Department of Literature, I assure you. It can't happen there," said Paul, determined to break free of the group, before they drained away every last bit of conviction that he had inside him.

This time he did manage to stride toward the university entrance, but if his outward appearance was confident, inwardly he was debating whether he had, indeed, done the right thing. He had no illusions about the students who were members of the German Students' Association, who were always on the lookout for an opportunity to start a fight. But then he recalled his meetings with Professor Laufer and the way that the professor had always treated him with kindness and respect. What was even more reassuring was that Laufer was built like a prize fighter, complete with a broken nose. If the thugs from the student group tried to start up with Laufer, they would be in for a surprise, Paul decided.

He had made it across the square without incident, and even though he chided himself for doing it, he let out a sigh of relief. He wondered if this was how the soldiers of the Great War had felt on the battlefield, grateful for every few yards they were able to traverse, still in one piece.

Then he was inside the front hall, which was surging with the press and sway of bodies and vibrating with noise. Was it more crowded than usual this morning, or had he never before noticed the din?

"Herr Hoffmann!" a voice called out.

It took Paul a few moments to discover where the voice had come from, since there were no familiar faces in his immediate vicinity.

"Here, Herr Hoffmann," said the voice, which belonged to a young man who was smiling. "We look forward to hearing your presentation."

Paul looked from the smiling student to his companion, who was also grinning. He was certain that he did not know them. "I hope you will not be disappointed, sirs," he said, giving each of them a slight bow, "but admittance is usually limited to students enrolled in the department."

"The university decided to make an exception for you, Herr Hoffmann," said the second student.

"The entire German Students' Association has been invited," said the other one.

"Then I hope you will enjoy it." Paul bowed stiffly and walked toward the staircase.

"I'm sure we will," said the second student to his friend, not bothering to hide his smirk.

Paul wasn't sure if it was his imagination or if the waves of students really did part like the Red Sea as he walked up the staircase, but he did make it to the top and down the corridor without further incident. His destination was a small waiting room that adjoined the lecture hall. He knocked on the closed door and waited.

"Herr Hoffmann?" asked the wizened attendant who opened the door.

The old man had probably admitted thousands of nervous students in his time, and Paul wondered how many, like him, had wondered if they were about to enter the gates of Heaven or Hell. But safely inside the waiting room he was, and there was nothing to do but wait.

The attendant had disappeared to somewhere, leaving Paul to commune with his thoughts. From the other side of the closed door that led to the lecture hall, he thought he could hear the droning hum of voices, many voices. He didn't necessarily mind the thought of defending his thesis before a room full of people — he had prepared for the hour as much as was humanly possible — but he wished he could be sure there would be at least one friendly face out there in the crowd. Then he chided himself for causing himself needless anxiety; Professor Laufer had practically written his thesis for him. That would be his friendly face, and since Laufer was chairman of the department it was the only friendly face he needed.

The attendant returned and asked Paul if he was ready. Paul heard himself say yes with more self-assurance than he would have thought possible just a few hours earlier.

"Very good, sir," said the attendant, opening the door that led to the lecture hall.

Through the open door, Paul could see much of the hall, which appeared to be full. The old man shuffled to the other side of the stage, where a table had been placed, and pounded some sort of gavel on the wood surface. The chatter immediately died down.

"Gentlemen, we are ready to begin. I present Herr Paul Hoffmann."

The attendant nodded to Paul, who took a deep breath and walked through the open door.

iii.

He had never been one to go in for amateur theatrics, and so he found the experience odd. There he was standing on the stage, arranging his papers on the lectern, pretending that he wasn't aware that perhaps one hundred pairs of eyes were upon him. He wondered how long he would have to go on shuffling through his papers; it seemed like a longish time had already gone by. Then he heard the attendant clear his throat and he realized that the man was waiting for him to signal that he was ready. He signaled and the attendant pounded on the table a second time.

"Gentlemen, I present the distinguished senior members of the faculty."

The students sitting in the audience stamped their feet loudly, as was the custom in German universities. Paul had always thought this was a strange way to show respect, but it was an ancient custom, or so he had been told during his first week of classes.

A second door, this one located at the opposite wall, opened and three senior professors entered, all looking very solemn. Professor Hurst was at the head of the procession, Paul noted, just as he observed that none of the men looked at him. *Guilty until proved innocent,* he said to himself, as he pretended to once again be busy with his papers.

After the three senior professors had taken their seats at the long table, the attendant took up his gavel for the third and final time. "Gentlemen and distinguished members of the faculty," he called out with a strength that was surprising in such an old man, "I present the chairman of the department, Herr Doktor Professor Laufer."

The stomping that followed surpassed what had gone before. To Paul's ears it sounded like a stampede of a thousand elephants, and again he wondered why this animal-like display should be an expression of honor.

The foot-stomping was still going strong when the door at the opposite end of the stage opened a second time. The doorway was empty for a moment, and Paul was once again reminded of the theatre. There were star actors who would not make their entrance until the audience was worked up to a frenzy of anticipation; perhaps the Herr Professor was emulating that example.

Then a man entered, and Paul let out an audible gasp. If the person had a face, he could not see it. All he could see was the costume that this person was wearing, the uniform of a Brown Shirt.

The stamping grew even louder, although now it was accompanied by cheers and whistles, as Professor Laufer — for it was the professor of literature who had exchanged his civilian dress for the uniform of the new Germany — walked to the table and took his seat at the head. Paul tried to catch the attention of the other three professors, but all of them, including Professor Hurst, were keeping their eyes studiously on the pads of paper that had been placed on the table beforehand, for their use.

Professor Laufer raised his hand, and the room grew quiet. In that gesture, Paul decided that he had been wrong; the professor was not an actor but a conductor, and the students sitting in the hall were his orchestra. What remained to be seen was what his role was in all this.

His eyes were once again glued to his thesis manuscript and, following the metaphor, by some trick of the eye the letters had turned into notes of music. He could hear the music, too. It had been playing on the radio program earlier that day: Beethoven's *Pathetique Sonata*. The sonata was a favorite choice for that sort of program, which was designed to appeal to a broad audience. Beethoven was always popular, and that particular piece gave the pianist an opportunity to display his virtuosity even while it gave the listener an opportunity to hum along, at least in the second movement.

And he had hummed along, there in his room, although now it seemed like a ridiculous thing to do. When a situation was truly "pathetic" one did not hum, he supposed. But, then, what did one do? Cry? Fall to one's knees and beg for mercy? Put a gun to one's head before others blew out your brains for you?

He recalled the words of Friedrich Schiller, words that the poet had written in his essay on the pathetic, words that

Paul would have liked to have discussed in his thesis on *Hamlet*, had he been given the chance. The depiction of suffering, as mere suffering, was not the purpose of art. It was the resistance to that suffering, resistance to the emotions of suffering, which was tragedy's aim. The "pathetic"—as a true act of the soul—was revealed only when the person first engaged in suffering, and then, in an act of moral freedom, declared his independence from pain or despair.

Perhaps, then, humming wasn't such a bad idea after all. But there was no longer time. Professor Laufer was speaking.

"Good morning, Herr Hoffmann."

"Good morning, Herr Doktor Professor Laufer, and other distinguished members of the faculty." Paul again tried to make eye contact with the other professors, but only Professor Laufer was willing to meet his eye.

"Pardon me, Herr Hoffmann—and gentlemen of the faculty and members of the student body—if I begin today's proceedings by stating an obvious fact. But the awarding of a degree from an institution as prestigious as the University of Berlin is a great responsibility. Would you agree with me, Herr Hoffmann?"

"Yes, Herr Doktor Professor," Paul replied.

"Are you sure, Herr Hoffmann?"

"Yes, very sure."

"And would you also agree that it is the task of the faculty to bestow a degree only upon those students whose academic work demonstrates that they understand the importance of the lofty task that awaits them—that it is they who will be the privileged interpreters of Germany's destiny, the intellectual standard bearers of the new political and social order that is Germany's futurity?"

Paul hesitated.

"Well, Herr Hoffmann?"

"I was only wondering, Herr Doktor Professor, if, that is, if I may respectfully ask a question, but my area of research is the literature of Elizabethan England. I am not sure I understand what Shakespeare has to do with Germany's destiny."

"I will explain, Herr Hoffmann. Would you not agree that William Shakespeare, although born in England, is a writer who is German in spirit? That, in fact, we could say that Herr Shakespeare is one of us?"

"Yes, I would agree with that."

"Would you also agree that although Shakespeare may be timeless, he has something relevant to say to Germans who are living today; that we can look to his plays for wisdom, inspiration, and guidance?"

"Yes."

"Then how is it that in your thesis you have turned Shakespeare into a subversive and an enemy of the State?"

"Where did I do that?" Paul blurted out. Then, regaining his composure, he said, "There has been some misunderstanding. Perhaps something I wrote wasn't clear."

"No, Herr Hoffmann, what you wrote is most clear. I will read it to you, and I quote, 'Antonio, the merchant who gives the play its name, is most certainly a trafficker in the slave trade; but even though we are meant to admire his good qualities, his kindness and generosity toward his friends, it is most certain that this should not be construed as approval on the part of Shakespeare of Antonio's involvement in the slave trade. Nor should we conclude that a humanist like William Shakespeare, who represents the apex of the enlightened spirit, would ever condone compelling any human being to perform forced and demeaning labor, which can only result in the dulling and degradation of the human soul.' Do you recognize this passage, Herr Hoffmann? Do you admit that these are your words?"

"Yes, I wrote that."

"And you believe that what you wrote is a true and accurate statement of Shakespeare's position on slave labor?"

"Yes, I do."

"Do you then also believe that the present government's policy of rehabilitating political opponents and social

~ 42 ~

undesirables through their compulsory participation in productive manual labor on behalf of the Fatherland is something that Shakespeare — whom you said just a few moments ago is one of us — would find objectionable? Is that your learned opinion, Herr Hoffmann, that if William Shakespeare were to walk into this room this moment, he would disagree with the policies of our government, which, by the way, have the approval of the vast majority of the German people?"

"But you said in March ..."

"And this is May."

They might have had a staring contest, to see who would blink first. But even though the future is always unknown, at that moment any reasonable person would have felt confident placing his bet on Professor Laufer — who had the university behind him, the Brown Shirt uniform upon him, and the members of the German Students' Association before him — to win. Paul, who despite his romantic notions did have a reasonable side, looked down at his thesis manuscript, whose pages seemed to have turned blank.

"I ... well, perhaps ... perhaps I did go too far to presume to speak for Shakespeare."

"Then speak for yourself. Are you aware, Herr Hoffmann, of the new law that will compel university students to engage in manual labor for a period of six months?"

"No, I was not aware of any such law."

"Well, now you are, and so my question to you is this: You, Herr Hoffmann, stand before us today and say, 'Approve my thesis. Give me my degree. Allow me to teach in Germany's universities, influence her young people, and mold their spirits and their minds.' But what, Herr Hoffmann, are you prepared to do in return for this great honor? Are you willing to be a role model, a standard bearer, and lead the way to Germany's destiny? Are you willing to sign your name to this piece of paper, and show your commitment to the Fatherland by agreeing to perform manual labor in the Dachau labor camp for the next six months?"

Paul stared at the piece of paper that Professor Laufer had shoved into his hands. The Dachau concentration camp had opened only in March, just a few months earlier, supposedly to rehabilitate political enemies of the Nazi regime. Not too much was known about what was going on inside the camp gates, but what was known about Nazi tactics on the open streets was enough to make Paul say, instinctively, "You must be mad."

The moment he said those four words, Paul knew that his fate had been sealed. He heard and he saw what followed, but it was as if he heard and saw it all from another place.

"Gentlemen," Professor Laufer was saying to the assembled students, "will you sit quietly while this Jewish subversive insults the honor of our university and its faculty?"

"No! No!" a few students shouted.

"Will you let him spit upon the laws of our country?"

"Stop him! Throw him out!" several more joined in.

"Is it only the Jew who has eyes and ears?" Professor Laufer was shouting. "If you wrong us, shall we not take revenge?"

At this signal, several students jumped onto the stage. One of them punched Paul in the mouth. The action sent him reeling across the stage, until he knocked against the table where the three senior members of the faculty were still seated. For a moment, he found himself staring Professor Hurst in the eye. Then he was lifted and carried out of the room.

Professor Shultz, who had been sitting in the audience, pushed against the tide of students and rushed up to Professor Laufer, who was watching the fracas from upstage. "Herr Doktor Professor, I wish to hand in my resignation."

"Accepted," Professor Laufer replied.

Professor Shultz ran out of the room and into the hallway. From the top of the stairs, he had an unobstructed view of the noisy procession, which had reached the building's entry hall. The students carrying Paul heaved his unresisting body back and forth several times, and then they threw him out of the front door.

Paul hit the pavement face first. He supposed he was hurt, but that wasn't why he didn't move. If he felt pain, it was first the pain of humiliation. Any physical pain he might feel later would be nothing in comparison.

He was still lying in the courtyard when he heard a voice calling to him. It sounded vaguely familiar.

"Herr Hoffmann! Up here!"

Paul managed to prop himself up on his elbow. He saw two students standing by an upper window.

"You forgot something, Herr Hoffmann," the second student called out. "Your thesis!"

The two students threw the manuscript out of the window. The unbound pages floated in the breeze like a flotilla of ships lazily headed toward dozens of distant ports. Paul raised himself to his knees and tried to catch the pages that were falling all around him.

One of the two students wrapped a page around a large rock and threw it from the window, aiming for the back of Paul's head. It was a direct hit.

HEAVEN

CHAPTER V

I t was a busy place, and large. Or so it seemed, as Paul was led through what seemed to be an endless maze of corridors, up some staircases and down some others. He still felt very weak after his recent ordeal, and so he didn't ask any questions. Besides, there was no one to ask. His guardian—or was it his jailer?—was always several steps in front of him and it was all Paul could do to keep up.

At last they came to a halt at some sort of waiting room, or at least Paul waited. His companion had disappeared behind a closed door. For the first time he was aware of a dull aching pain at the back of his head. He also felt something cold and damp trickling down the side of his neck. He reached into his suit jacket pocket for a handkerchief and noticed that the jacket's lining had gotten torn. When he wiped his face with his handkerchief he saw that the white cloth had turned red. A further examination revealed that his trousers were dirty, as was the front of his shirt, and his leather shoes were scuffed.

He wished there were a wash basin in the room, and a mirror, so that he could clean away the blood and dirt. He assumed he was about to be interviewed by someone, and he wanted to look presentable and not like some undesirable who had rolled in off the street. When his warden re-entered the room he was about to ask if there was a lavatory nearby, but before he knew it he was standing inside a large room and he heard the door close behind him.

The room seemed to be an office. The walls were lined with several bookcases, which were filled with hundreds of tall leather-bound volumes. There were also several metal filing cabinets that stretched from floor to ceiling, and if the one half-open drawer was any sign the cabinets were stuffed to overflowing with official dossiers.

In the center of the room was a long rectangle table, worn with age, at which sat three elderly men. They were dressed alike, from their snowy-white beards to their raven-colored robes. There were also two other men in the room, who were dressed in business suits, as befitted a modern professional. They each had their own table, and they sat opposite one another, in adversarial fashion. Off to the side was yet another table, smaller in size, when a non-descript man sat hunched over a typewriter, punching the keys with a steady rhythm; this man was some kind of secretary or stenographer, Paul supposed.

As for Paul, he was standing in the center of the room, although why he did not know. No one was paying attention to him; instead all five heads were buried in the papers that sat on the tables. Finally, after what seemed to be an eternity, one of the elderly men looked up.

"Do you know why you are here, Herr Hoffmann?" he asked.

"No, sir."

"You have received a serious blow to the head, and your life is hanging in the balance. It is the responsibility of this Heavenly Court to determine if there is a compelling reason why your life should be saved."

"My life?" Paul looked at the elderly man and the other faces; if this was a joke they were hiding it very well.

"Should the Court discover that you have not yet fulfilled your purpose in life, you will be returned to the world below," the elderly judge continued. "If, however, the Court finds that you have fulfilled that purpose—or that the time allotted to your stay on earth has elapsed—your case will be sent to the Higher Court for final judgment."

"But surely there's no question. I'm still young."

Paul noticed that the two other judges were trying to hide their smiles. He wasn't aware that he had said anything that was amusing.

"My colleagues are smiling because age is just one factor among many," said the elderly judge. "Some souls fulfill their earthly purpose in a week; others must strive and toil for tens of thousands of days. Now, Herr Hoffmann, if you are ready, the deposition will begin. The gentleman to your left is the prosecuting attorney, and the gentleman to your right has been appointed by the Court to act in your defense."

The lawyer for the prosecution rose from his seat with an unhurried air of importance. After acknowledging the three judges and the opposing counsel, he turned to Paul and said, "Herr Hoffmann, a moment ago you implied that you have not yet fulfilled your purpose in the world below. Could you please tell the Court what you think that purpose is?"

Paul tried to focus on the question, but it was difficult. He had a vague recollection of sitting in a café with his friend Meyer and discussing that very topic, but for the life of him he couldn't remember what he had said. If only his head weren't throbbing like a jackhammer. He wondered if there was a doctor on the premises, or if anyone in the room had a bottle of aspirin. Then it came back to him, vaguely, the conversation in the café. Meyer was going to be a doctor; he was going to heal people's bodies. And Paul was going to heal people's souls.

"I intend to become a professor of literature," he said with confidence, now that the earlier conversation was fresh in his mind. "I hope to pass on to future generations an appreciation for the masterpieces of Western culture and the humanistic principles that they espouse."

"Anything else?"

"Well, if my own poetry — that is, the poetry that I intend one day to write — should find a place in that canon, I shouldn't mind."

"Anything else?"

"No, I don't think so."

The prosecuting attorney leafed through some pages in his folder and then extracted one of them. After adjusting his pince-nez and quickly perusing the text written upon the page, he looked up at Paul, smiled, and said, "Herr Hoffmann, you mentioned the words 'Western culture.' I presume that you consider this culture to be something worthy of your life's devotion."

"Of course," Paul replied. "The study of Shakespeare, Schiller—what could be more elevating, more ennobling than that?"

"You admire the writings of Herr Schiller very much, don't you?"

"What German doesn't?"

"Very true. What German doesn't? And yet, I have here in my hand a letter that Herr Schiller wrote—it is Letter V of his *Letters Upon the Aesthetic Education of Man*—and in it, after he discusses the problems afflicting the lower, uneducated classes, he writes, and I quote, 'On the other hand, the civilized classes give us the still more repulsive sight of lethargy, and of a depravity of character which is the more revolting because it roots in culture. I forget who of the older or more recent philosophers makes the remark, that what is more noble is the more revolting in its destruction. The remark applies with truth to the world of morals. The child of nature, when he breaks loose, becomes a madman; but the art scholar, when he breaks loose, becomes a debased character. The enlightenment of the understanding, on which the more refined classes pride themselves with some ground, shows on the whole so little of an ennobling influence on the mind that it seems rather to confirm corruption by its maxims.' Are you familiar with these words, Herr Hoffmann?"

"I am, but Schiller was writing after the French Revolution. He was appalled by the violence, as any cultured person would be, and by the failure of the Revolution to put its ideals into practice. But it would be false to say that

Schiller was against culture. In fact, he wrote, in his letters, that it was possible to elevate the moral character of a people through a society based upon aesthetic ideals."

"And yet he writes, and again I quote, 'Culture, far from giving us freedom, only develops, as it advances, new necessities; the fetters of the physical close more tightly around us, so that the fear of loss quenches even the ardent impulse toward improvement, and the maxims of passive obedience are held to be the highest wisdom of life. Thus the spirit of the time is seen to waver between perversions and savagism, between what is unnatural and mere nature, between superstition and moral unbelief, and it is often nothing but the equilibrium of evils that sets bounds to it.' Where is this elevation that you speak of, Herr Hoffmann? Where is the ennobling of the soul, or as you would have it, the elevation of the moral character of a people?"

"Again, Schiller was speaking about his own age. But in his writings, he envisioned a future ideal state, one where the principles of aesthetic beauty would open the mind and the heart and turn them to the good. He envisioned a new civilization where people would be content and where life would be beautiful."

"Would you say that Germany has reached that ideal state and that life in Germany in the year 1933 is beautiful?"

"Even Schiller admitted that his aesthetic state was more utopian than practical. But the hope remains."

"Hope—another interesting word. Herr Hoffmann, I have here in my notes a transcription of a conversation that you had not long ago with a friend of yours called Meyer Aronstein, and you said, 'The world calls me a Jew, and yet I don't identify with anything Jewish.' Yet in this very room you have just now mentioned the concept of 'hope.' Are you not aware that the idea of hope and a better world are Jewish concepts; that it was the Jews who first rejected the idea that time is cyclical and repetitive and that the human individual lacks the ability to progress, and, instead, introduced the concept of linear time and the possibility of repairing the world and reaching a future where the world would achieve its perfection?"

"I'm afraid that I don't know very much about Jewish history."

"That is surprising, given your interest in Shakespeare and Schiller and the notion of the sublime."

"I do not see the connection."

"Did not Schiller write, 'One can display magnificence in good fortune, but sublimity only in misfortune'?"

"I still do not see the connection."

"Let me explain, then. If a person were to study the history of the German or the English people, he might be impressed by the magnificence of those peoples' culture— their literature and their music, their philosophy and expression of humanistic ideals. But, according to Schiller's statement, one could not call that culture sublime. Although it is true that every nation has seen its share of war and social upheaval, nevertheless, it is also true that it was the good fortune of those people to live in their own land uninterrupted for centuries; they had time to develop their own language, create their own worldview—they had at their disposal a kneading trough, so to speak, where their culture could be molded and shaped and then left to ferment, until the time arrived when it reached a state of magnificence and could create a Shakespeare or a Schiller, a Beethoven or a Bach. Jewish history, on the other hand, has been for the past two thousand years a history of misfortune, a history of exile and expulsion, a history of chaos and cruelty. And yet the Jew has confronted that history without fear; he has preserved his independence. He has been tested in every generation, and in every generation he has emerged with his inner freedom intact. Is that not proof that he is sublime, according to the definition expounded by Herr Schiller?"

"Perhaps one could make an argument for the general case, if what you say is indeed the truth."

"What about the individual? Take a Jew like Shylock, for instance; could he be an example of the sublime?"

"I do not believe so."

"You have studied the issue?"

"There is no need to. Everyone knows that Shylock is despicable."

"Everyone? How does 'everyone' know? Upon what does your 'everyone' base his opinion? Ignorance? Prejudice? Passive obedience to the spirit of the time?"

"I will concede that there have been some misguided actors and literary critics who have attempted to portray Shylock as more sinned against than sinning," said Paul, "but their argument falls apart once you read the play. No one in their right mind would say that Shylock is Shakespeare's favorite child, or even one that he felt a fondness for."

"And yet is it not possible to say that Shylock is not entirely despised, either? During the trial scene, Shylock could have killed Antonio in a fit of frenzy, but he does not. He will not go so far; his hatred has a limit. Can that, at least, not be said in Shylock's defense?"

"If I may ask a question," said Paul, "is it Shylock who is on trial here, or me?"

"The question is a valid one," said the elderly judge. "The Court asks the prosecuting attorney to get to the point. Brevity can also be sublime."

"Very well," said the attorney. "Herr Hoffmann, in your thesis, 'Shakespeare and *The Banished Heart*,' you claimed, based upon your research — or, rather, research that Professor Hurst put at your disposal — that Shylock, as originally conceived by Shakespeare, was to have been a tragic figure rooted in the sublime; that Shakespeare at first intended to write a very different play, but he changed his mind after he was hired by the Earl of Essex to rabble-rouse for the Earl, whose political ambitions were enormous and who was willing to stop at nothing — not even the murder of an innocent man — to achieve them. Is that not correct?"

When Paul did not reply, the prosecuting lawyer took up a stack of papers in his hand and shook them vaguely in Paul's direction. "You do recall writing a thesis?"

"Yes, I wrote a thesis, but not that one."

"Why not?"

"What does it matter? Dr. Lopez is dead. Even if I had written that thesis, he would still be dead."

"But did you not consider what impact the thesis might have had on your own times? Is it not true that Shakespeare's Shylock has poisoned the minds of countless people throughout the generations, including the people in Germany in the year 1933? Did you not consider that you might have been able to correct this distorted view of Shylock, and the entire Jewish people, by revealing the truth about the writing of this play and Shakespeare's own rather sordid part in perpetuating an image of the Jew that he personally knew to be a lie?"

"The topic didn't interest me. Is that a crime?"

The prosecuting attorney smiled. "That is for the Court to decide."

The attorney re-took his seat at his desk. Paul was aware of a blessed silence that had descended upon the room; the typist had momentarily rested his hands upon the table, silencing the relentless clacking of his machine. In the pause, Paul tried to find some signs of reassurance from the others. Surely, he wasn't the only one who saw no relevance in the questions that he had been asked. But the faces of the three judges were impassive while they waited for the lawyer for the defense to begin, which he did without further delay.

"Herr Hoffmann, forgive me if I state the obvious, but the Jews of Germany have entered into a difficult period of their history. Would you agree with that statement?"

"I suppose so."

"What is not so obvious for someone like you, who lives according to the rules of earthly, sequential time, is that Germany's Jews are about to confront a terrifying raging maelstrom the like of which not even your Schiller could imagine. As for you, Herr Hoffmann, you will no longer be able to say, as you said in the office of Professor Hurst, that you do nothing as a Jew. In a very short time you will not be able to do anything as a German. You will not be able to teach in German schools. You will not be able to publish your poems in German periodicals. You will not even be able to sit in a German park or drink coffee in a German café. Anything you do, you will have to do as a Jew, and a ridiculed and despised Jew at that. So the question is this: Do you see yourself as playing a role in this new chapter of Jewish history?"

"I ... I don't know."

"Come, Herr Hoffmann, you have many talents. You have intelligence, a gift for language. Granted it won't be easy after your mask of German culture is stripped away, but even Schiller learned to repudiate the confused errors that marred his youthful thinking. Goethe, as well, regretted the literary work of his youth and the fatal passion of his young Werther, whose love for that which was not his to obtain led to his destruction. Goethe in life had the good sense to do what his literary hero could not, and find a new reason for existence. Surely you can do the same and imagine some sort of new life for yourself."

When Paul was silent, the lawyer continued, "For instance, could you not find a way to retrieve that manuscript that Professor Laufer intends to destroy and make its contents available to the public?"

"I object," said the prosecuting attorney, rising to his feet. "The lawyer for the defense is leading the witness."

"Sustained," said the elderly judge. "Please try to be more careful with how you phrase your questions."

"What did he get a *klop* on the head for, if not to wake him up?" asked the lawyer for the defense.

"Even so, the witness must provide his own proof for his defense."

The elderly judge motioned to the prosecuting attorney to sit down and for the lawyer for the defense to proceed. He then said to Paul, "Would you like to answer the last question? The Court stenographer will repeat the last line, to refresh your memory."

The Court stenographer read from his typewritten page, in a flat, uninterested voice, "Surely you can do the same and imagine some sort of new life for yourself."

Paul, sensing a sympathetic ear in the elderly judge, directed his answer to him. "I couldn't write that thesis about *The Banished Heart*. If I had written it, I would have been thrown out of the university. My career would have been over."

"And so you therefore decided to sacrifice the truth?"

Paul was silent.

"Was it worth it, Herr Hoffmann?" asked the judge. "In the end, you know, you were thrown out of the university. Your career is over."

"What could I do?"

"The past is finished. The question the Court is interested in pertains to the future: What can you do?"

Paul stared down at his hands. He saw the blood-stained handkerchief, which he was still holding, as well as the torn piece of lining that was hanging from the bottom of his jacket. He saw the dirty trousers, the scuffed shoes. He imagined his face was an unholy sight, as well. He did not know this person, this dirty, disheveled person; and he did not want to know this person. He did not want to be a person who lay sprawled in the courtyard of a German university, while a crowd of his peers stood around him and jeered. He did not want to be a person whose beliefs were scorned and whose work was rejected. He did not want such a life, and he refused to be convinced that such a life could be sublime, as the prosecuting attorney had seemed to suggest.

"What can you do, Herr Hoffmann?"

Paul shook his head, his thoughts still focused on that figure that was lying face down in the courtyard of the University of Berlin, the blood trickling down the side of his neck. "Nothing."

"Thank you, Herr Hoffmann," said the elderly judge. "The Court is dismissed."

The folders were snapped shut with dizzying speed. The noise caused something to snap in Paul's mind, as well. The image in the university courtyard disappeared and he was suddenly acutely aware that the judges and lawyers were preparing to leave.

"Dismissed?" Paul shouted out, trying to get the attention of the elderly judge who sat at the head of the table.

"Yes, we will send your file upstairs for final judgment."

"Final ... That isn't fair!"

"Isn't fair? That's a very serious accusation to bring against a Heavenly Court."

"This trial has been a farce! I'm a German! What did you expect me to say? That I'll go enroll in some yeshivah or sail to Palestine and pick oranges for the rest of my life?"

"We expected nothing except the truth, Herr Hoffmann," said the elderly judge. "And we appreciate your answering the questions with such candor."

"But you didn't let me present a defense — my defense. That thesis, 'Shakespeare and *The Banished Heart*,' where are the parts of the thesis that I did write? Why has that not been admitted as evidence?"

"You wrote part of this thesis?"

"Not exactly finished text, but I did do some research and ... and made a few notes. Where is that?"

The elderly judge looked in the folder, which was still sitting on the table, and leafed through the pages. "I am afraid there isn't much here, Herr Hoffmann; just a few jottings, a few ideas."

"Ideas, that's right! It's all in my head."

"What is all in your head?" asked the prosecuting attorney. "Are you telling the Court that you remember what was written in that manuscript and are prepared to reveal the truth about William Shakespeare and the writing of this play?"

"Yes. I could write the thesis now, if ... if only I had ... time."

There were a few more clacks from the typewriter and then once again a silence descended upon the room. Everyone waited for the elderly judge to pronounce his sentence.

"All right," he said at last, putting the blank pages of the manuscript on the table. "Sit down, Herr Hoffmann, sit down."

While Paul took a seat at the table, a clerk entered the room, carrying an hourglass, which he placed on the table, next to the manuscript. The elderly judge lifted the hourglass and turned it over, so that grains of sand began to flow into the empty half of the glass.

"We'll give you time."

STRATFORD

CHAPTER VI

It is unlikely that anyone paid too much attention when a new family moved into Stratford-upon-Avon in the year 1570. The head of the family, John Rivers, brewer, was a dour-looking widower, although he was still only in his mid-thirties. His son Henry was an ordinary six-year-old child and hardly a figure to attract notice, and the same could be said for an infant daughter named Joan. Old Isaac, the grandfather of John's recently deceased wife and great-grandfather to Henry and Joan, was the sort of doddering old man that one often saw sitting before the hearth, where he mumbled garbled reminiscences of days gone by; in short, he was also the type of person who could be comfortably ignored. Therefore, we may excuse the generations of historians who, in their zeal to uncover scraps of information concerning Stratford's favorite and most famous son, have totally overlooked a family that was to play such an important role in Shakespeare's life.

But to return to our story, for we shall not make the same mistake as others, on this particular day several laborers were hard at work removing heavy pieces of household furniture and goods from a wagon and carrying them into the half-timbered, two-story house that recently had been purchased by John Rivers for himself and his family.

A gaggle of local children, who, having nothing better to do, had come to see the show, but they were quickly scared away when John shouted out to them, "Go home, you young rascals! Shoo! Get out of the men's way."

They all ran off. Only one of them bothered to return, a six-year-old boy named William, who could often be found in places where he wasn't wanted and shouldn't be found, due to his insatiable curiosity about almost every topic. In truth, though, William wasn't only interested in the cupboards and trunks that were being carried inside. He had immediately spotted the boy who belonged to those trunks and was wondering if this new arrival to his town would be a friend or foe.

Meanwhile, John Rivers, who had been successful in his business and was used to command, was busy directing the movements of the laborers, instructing this one to put the heavy carved wooden chairs in the downstairs front room, and the packing case filled with dishes and pots in the kitchen located in the back.

"Where does this go, sir?" asked one of the men, who had loaded a beaten-looking trunk onto his back.

John did not recognize it as one of his own; it therefore must have belonged to Old Isaac. "Take it upstairs," he instructed the man. "Put it in the small room at the back."

It suddenly occurred to John that he hadn't seen Old Isaac for some time. He therefore called out to Henry, "Where is your grandfather?"

"I don't know."

"Go find him. I don't want him wandering off."

Henry went round to the back of the house, studiously avoiding going too near to the place off to the side where a gnarled and leafy tree had taken root. He had seen a boy hidden in one of the tree's lower boughs and, like William — for it was William who had positioned himself in the tree, where he thought he could observe without being observed but was actually hidden only to himself — he was unsure if that boy was merely spying out the land or intended to wage war.

There was a garden in the back of the house, which had become overgrown. But it was not so overgrown that it could hide a grandfather, and so Henry thought to return to the front of the house and explore the nearby streets.

"I know where he is," said William, who had left his leafy perch and followed Henry to the garden. "I saw him from the tree."

"Will you tell me where he went?"

While the two boys were negotiating the terms of the exchange of information, John had come round to the garden. He was not pleased to see Henry talking to the other child. "He will give you nothing, you young good-for-nothing," he said to William. "But I will give you a box on the ears if you do not leave my property at once. "

"I am not a good-for-nothing, sir. I am the son of John Shakespeare, and he will give you a box on the ears if you do not learn to speak more politely to his son."

William did not wait to see how the man would respond, but ran off as quick as his legs could carry him.

John glared at Henry and spat out a slew of questions. "What did that boy want? Did he ask you your name? What did you tell him?"

"I didn't tell him anything. He didn't ask."

"But he will. He'll be back, the nosy brat, and when he does come back what will you say?"

"I'll say my name is Henry, Henry Rivers, like you told me to."

"And when he asks where you come from?"

"I'll say … I'll say …"

"You'll say what, boy?" John Rivers demanded.

Old Isaac, who was clasping to his sunken chest the baby, who was swaddled in linen cloth and drooling merrily all over his aged jerkin, came to his great-grandson's rescue. "Don't shout, John, unless you want everyone in Stratford to hear you."

John grumbled under his breath. It had been a long day and he was tired—and he was angry that he had forgotten himself, and done it while Old Isaac was watching. But he was not the sort of man who could admit that he was wrong, and so he said, "I don't know why it's so hard for you two to remember that our name is Rivers and we're from Yorkshire."

"Maybe it would be easier to remember if our name really was Rivers and we really were from that place," Old Isaac replied.

Henry, despite his better judgment—and life and its misfortunes had made him wise beyond his years—laughed. He and his grandfather were allies, much to the chagrin of John Rivers, who looked upon the old man as a burden, and a dangerous one at that.

"From now on, you're to stay in your room and keep your mouth shut," John said to the old man. "And if that doesn't suit your fancy, you can go back to London and fend for yourself."

"I'd do it, if it weren't for the boy and this little girl," Old Isaac replied. "They're the only family I have left in the world, and that's a sorry thing for an old man like me to say."

"It's no fault of mine that you refused to follow my wife and the other children to the grave."

"You're a harsh man, Judah. You always were."

"John! John Rivers is my name now. And my son's name is Henry. You'd better remember it."

"Henry. What sort of name is Henry?"

"It's a name that's good enough for the kings of England."

"Kings of England, kings of Spain, they're all a rotten lot."

John grabbed the elderly man and shook him. "Have you gone mad?"

"Mind the child," Old Isaac replied, freeing himself from the younger man's grip to protect the baby girl, who had started to cry. "I regret the day I allowed you to marry my only grandchild. It's you who sent her to an early grave. You broke her heart."

"She died of the plague, along with the other children," John replied. "And why that plague spared you, instead of ..."

The sound of a loud crash inside the house caused John to forget Old Isaac for the moment. He rushed to the front of the house and through the open front door, while the others followed. Their eyes were greeted by the sight of one of the laborers, who had been hauling Old Isaac's heavy trunk up the stairs, staring open-mouthed and displaying his missing front tooth to whoever chose to see it. While the man had made it safely to the top of the stairs, the trunk had escaped from his hands and tumbled down to the entryway. During the journey the top had come open and the trunk's contents were strewn all over the floor.

John looked with alarm at Old Isaac's escaped treasure — Hebrew books, a prayer shawl, silver candlesticks, and other items pertaining to Jewish ritual.

"I'm sorry, sir," said the laborer. "I tripped and the trunk slipped out of my hands. I'll clean it all up."

"No! Go back upstairs. Help the others finish unpacking the chest in the front bedroom."

When the workman had disappeared into an upstairs room, John picked up one of the fallen books, glanced at its pages, and said, "A Hebrew prayer book? You dared to bring all this? I tell you, Isaac, once those men leave this house it is all going straight into the fire."

"No, I beg of you," pleaded Old Isaac, all traces of his earlier bravado vanished. "Don't do it, please ... John."

Henry, who understood only that his father and grandfather were again quarreling, had already begun to put his grandfather's things back inside the trunk. He worked quickly and wordlessly, carefully avoiding the eyes of both his father and his grandfather. Soon all that remained outside the trunk was the prayer book. Henry did not ask for it. Instead, he waited by the trunk, with his eyes fixed upon his father's hand.

"Nothing in this trunk ever leaves your room, do you understand, Isaac?" John tossed the prayer book into the trunk. "And if I ever catch you filling my son's head with your religious superstitions, I'll throw you out of my house quicker than you can say Spanish Inquisition."

ii.

Six years passed, and by the end of them the Rivers family had become an established, if unremarked, presence in Stratford. John had remarried. His wife was a young woman from Stratford named Mary and she brought to the marriage a feather bed, a little property, and a great secret—she was a Catholic—which John magnanimously agreed to both forgive and guard with his life. Within the year Henry and Joan had a little brother, who was baptized and given the name James, which caused Old Isaac to mutter, "Another English king in the family. That's just what we need."

Old Isaac had not attended the baptism ceremony in the church. Instead, he had slipped away to a little one-room cottage he had found abandoned in the nearby woods. Despite John's command that he should stay in his room, after John had remarried he hadn't minded Old Isaac's daily forays into the countryside. Indeed, John wouldn't have minded if Old Isaac had taken up permanent residence in the cottage. The brewer had found contentment with his second wife and his new life as a respected Christian, and he was most happy when there was nothing to remind him that the life he was living in Stratford was a complete lie.

But the old man's health was declining and on some days he was too weak to attend to his own needs. Fortunately, the unsuspecting Mary didn't mind taking care of the old man, and she was too much a Christian to understand the occasional "superstitions" that slipped through Old Isaac's lips.

~ 65 ~

After the baptism ceremony, John and Mary hosted a festive meal in their home, to which many of the town's worthies were invited. It was a crowded, noisy gathering and Henry correctly guessed that a short absence on his part wouldn't be noticed. He therefore went to the kitchen, packed some food into a large handkerchief, and slipped out the back door.

Soon he had left behind the bustling streets of the town and was racing through the fields, hooting at the birds and dancing with the butterflies, which gave him a merry chase all the way to the abandoned cottage. So as not to startle his grandfather, who did not allow any visitors to enter his secluded kingdom except Henry, the boy knocked on the door first three times, and then five times, and then seven times, according to their pre-arranged signal. Old Isaac unbolted the door, and Henry stepped inside.

The cottage was of the old-fashioned and poorer kind. Perhaps it had been built for some woodsman or gamekeeper, whose needs were simple. At any rate, only one small window admitted a little light and fresh air into the gloomy room, which was shod with a dirt floor and crowned with a roof of thatch. A few pieces of antique furniture—a roughly hewn table and a bench and two stools, as well as a rickety bed—had been left behind by the previous owner. The hearth was in working order, and on cold days Old Isaac would light a small fire. On other days, he would bring out his prized possession, a bit of tallow, and use the candle to provide light.

It usually took Henry a few moments to adjust his eyes to the darkness, especially when the sun outside was bright, but that was only a momentary discomfort. He did not care that the cottage was dark and uncomfortable; his grandfather's presence provided the warmth and light that was missing from the grander family home in Stratford.

Henry opened the handkerchief and shared with his grandfather the morsels of food that he had brought from the kitchen. Old Isaac had some ale stored in the cottage, which he brought to the table, and so the two were quite content with their feast.

"Why didn't you come to the church, Grandfather?"

"How old are you now, Henry?"

Henry, who was used to his grandfather answering his questions by asking one of his own, replied, "I'll be twelve next month."

"You're almost a man."

"I should say I am."

"Are you old enough, then, to keep a secret? And before you answer, think carefully. Would you be able to keep a secret even if you were put on the rack and all the Queen's spy masters prodded and pulled at you to make you speak?"

"I can't say," Henry replied. "I'm not so very fond of being in pain."

"That's an honest answer. Let me then ask you another question. Can you keep a secret from your father and his new wife?"

"I already do."

"You do?"

"I know what you are."

"Do you?"

"Sometimes in the morning I watch you, through the keyhole, when you're wrapped in that big white shawl. You sway back and forth and move your lips very fast. Like this …"

Henry stood up and began to sway back and forth, while he mimed holding a book in his hands. Old Isaac watched the performance, not entirely happy with what he saw.

"So, you already know."

"But don't worry, Grandfather, I won't tell anyone that you are a wizard."

"A wizard?"

"You mean you're not?"

"No, of course not."

"Then you're a Catholic, like the rest of us?"

"No."

"You're a Protestant?"

"No."

Henry, having run out of guesses, looked at his grandfather with an expression of great puzzlement. "Then what are you?"

"I'm a Jew, Henry."

"A Jew?"

"So is your father. So was your mother. And so are you, and little Joan."

"That's impossible. My schoolmaster says there aren't any Jews in England. You only see Jews in plays. They wear red wigs and have big red noses."

"I can't vouch for the wigs, but officially your schoolmaster is right. You see, when our family was banished from Spain ..."

"Spain? But Spain is England's sworn enemy. Our family can't be from Spain."

Old Isaac gave his grandson a reassuring pat on the arm and refilled the boy's glass. "Don't worry, Henry, I have no love for the Spaniards, not after what they did to us. I was just a boy at the time. Would you like to hear the story?"

Henry was torn. He dearly loved stories, and he knew that no one told a story better than his grandfather. But he wasn't sure if he should listen to a good story about Spain, when his English sense of patriotism was warning him that there was nothing good about Spain, not even a story. However, his curiosity—which was matched only by one other boy in the town, his friend William Shakespeare, for the boys had become friends, seated as they were, side by side, in the Stratford grammar school—ruled, and he told his grandfather that he would like to hear the tale.

However, the moment had passed. Old Isaac's thoughts were very far away, and he seemed not to hear Henry's voice. Instead, he was hearing the voice of a different boy, a young child, who was standing on a Spanish pier and looking out to sea, where a ship was sailing away, and crying out, "Mama! Mama!"

"Grandfather, are you not feeling well?" Henry asked.

Old Isaac roused himself. "Don't worry, Henry. I'm fine."

"What about the story?"

"Some other time. You should be getting back home, before your father and step-mother miss you."

"But I still don't understand. Our family's secret is that we're Catholics. How can we be both Catholics and Jews?"

"Your step-mother is the true Catholic. But our family — your father, your poor deceased mother, and me — we were forced to convert to Catholicism, to save our lives. We only pretend to be good Christians. But in our hearts, we still consider ourselves to be Jews."

"Even my father?"

"No, perhaps not your father. I am afraid he banished our ancient faith from his heart not long after you were born. That was his decision, and it broke your mother's heart. When we moved here to Stratford, your father was determined that you would never know about your Jewish heritage. I agreed to keep it a secret, as long as you were a child. But in another year you will be considered an adult, according to the Jewish faith. You'll become responsible for your actions. I can no longer let you remain in ignorance. If you should choose to reject your people and your heritage, I cannot stop you. But I ask that before you make such a momentous decision that you first learn something about what it means to be a Jew, so that your decision will be based upon knowledge and not prejudice and ignorance."

"Who will be my teacher?"

"I will, may the One Above give me wisdom and strength. We'll learn together for just an hour every day. Then, on your thirteenth birthday, you can make your decision to either be a Jew, albeit in secret, or cast your lot with the Christians. Well, what do you say? Will you do it, if not for me then for the memory of your dear mother?"

Henry looked about him. The room had changed. Whereas before it had been a semi-magical place, a place where he was sure his grandfather practiced his magic arts, now he saw only a crumbling chamber that was dimly lit and poorly furnished. It had no allure, no promise of adventure, no hint of delightful secrets that might one day be his. The secrets that the room did promise to reveal were dark ones, heavy to bear and weary to hold. Even the thought of his mother did not lighten the burden. He barely remembered her or anything about that earlier life, except the terror that had entered their home, along with the plague. Yet he was not ready to sever the bond that he had with his grandfather—which he knew would happen if he refused the hour of study. A gulf of silence would stand between them, as it did between his grandfather and his father. He therefore said, "Yes, Grandfather, I'll do it."

"Thank you, Henry. But remember, this is a private matter between you, me and God. No one else must know. No one."

CHAPTER VII

Henry proved to be an apt student. Just as he had mastered his Latin and Greek at the grammar school, he was soon adept at deciphering basic Hebrew texts. As his proficiency grew, so did his desire to learn and the one hour spent on his Jewish studies sometimes expanded to several, especially during the summer, when the sunlight lingered into the evening hours.

But if Henry was happily employed after school, his friend William Shakespeare was not. It was not that William lacked imagination; he had plenty of that. But without a willing accomplice to assist with his pranks, laugh at his antics, and applaud his genius, life had lost some of its luster. The visit of a third-rate touring theatre company presenting a morality play temporarily improved his spirits. The actors were wondrously entertaining, as were the threadbare costumes and the stage machinery that went awry. There was the angel, for instance, dressed all in pearly gray — for it had been many years since the robe and wings had been white — who, while awaiting his entrance at the end of the play, passed the time by chewing tobacco and spitting the juice, with astounding accuracy, at the stray cats. When William, who found the offstage chatter more interesting than the pious talk onstage, asked the angel where he had acquired this feat, the heavenly being revealed that in a previous life he had been a seaman and sailed with John Hawkins across the ocean, where the tobacco plant grew in abundance.

After the troupe went on its way, Stratford life resumed its dull routine and William was restless. When his friend

Henry rebuffed yet again his invitation to recreate the Battle of Hastings on a nearby lawn, insisting that he had other business, William decided to find out what, exactly, that business was. Exchanging his imaginary soldier's garb for that of one of Her Majesty's spies, he stealthily followed Henry through field and grove, and watched, from a distance, as Henry slipped inside a snug and secluded cottage.

Now this was an interesting situation. William was sure that he could think of a thousand reasons—all of them thrilling—why a person might visit such a cottage, if he put his mind to it. But why should he tax his intellectual faculties? The cottage had a good thatch roof to climb upon—to spy through the window was too dangerous, for he could easily be discovered—and a few moments later he was removing bits of straw from his nose and trying not to sneeze, while finding his balance on his sloping perch.

When he felt that his foothold was secure, he carefully lifted up a small patch of the roof near the hole that let out the smoke from the hearth and looked down into the room. He saw Henry seated at a table beside his grandfather, whose snow-white beard and hair made him look old enough to be in heaven even without an angel's costume. William could also see an open book that sat upon the table, and in an instant his jealousy was aroused. Henry's grandfather was telling him stories! And Henry knew that William loved stories, too! This was no way to treat a friend!

William raised the bit of thatch a little higher, and called out, "Whaaaaooooooo," imitating the ghostly voice he had heard one of the actors use at the theatre troupe's performance.

Henry and Old Isaac heard the wail and looked uneasily about the room and at each other.

"What was that, I wonder?" Old Isaac muttered.

"It can't be an owl," said Henry. "It's still light. Perhaps it's a cuckoo."

William, chagrined that his ghost had been mistaken for a cuckoo, called out again, this time with more force, "Whaaaaaaaaaaaaaaaooooooooooooo!"

"It seems to be coming from the roof," said Henry, peering upward. "What can it be? Do you know, Grandfather?"

"I've never heard such a noise before in my life," Old Isaac replied.

"Whaaaaaooooo!" William called out again, very pleased with the effect that his wails were having. "I am the ghost of Old Isaac's father."

Old Isaac looked up with alarm, to William's delight.

"A ghost?" asked the old man, torn between belief and skepticism. "If you truly are the restless spirit of my departed father, give me some sign. Tell me what you want."

Since William had no idea what sort of sign to give, he went straight to the second request. "Why are you so mean, Grandfather Isaac? Why don't you ever invite William Shakespeare to your cottage and tell him stories? Whaaaooo ... Oooooh! Help! Help!"

Old Isaac sprang up from the bench. "That's no ghost! Come, Henry, let's see the wildcat that is making all this howling."

When they came outside, they discovered William, who had slid from his perch halfway down the roof, hanging on for dear life to a clump of thatch, while his legs dangled in the air.

"William Shakespeare! Well, this is much ado about nothing. What are you doing there?"

"Help me, Granddad! Help me, please!"

Old Isaac positioned himself so that he was below the boy, ready to catch him. "When I count to three, William, let yourself fall. Ready?"

William looked down and gave a half-hearted nod.

"One! Two! Three! Fall!"

William let go of the thatch and fell into Old Isaac's arms. The weight was too much for the old man, and the two of them collapsed onto the ground. But neither was hurt and, with Henry's aid, they were soon both standing on their feet.

"Now then, young man, what's this all about?" asked Old Isaac, trying to keep a stern look on his face.

"He's a spy!" said Henry. "Father must have sent him."

"Nobody sent me," protested William.

"Then what are you doing here?" asked Henry. "Why are you spying on us? I thought we were friends."

"We are friends, and that's why it's not fair."

"What's not fair?" asked Old Isaac.

"It's not fair that Henry comes here every day and the two of you sit together with a book and you tell Henry stories. I like stories, too. Why don't you ever tell Henry to invite me to come along?"

"You know, William, I believe you are right," said Old Isaac. "A grave injustice has been done. What shall we do?"

"We must go inside and correct it," William replied.

The other two followed William into the cottage, just in time to see William lift up the book that had sat upon the table but too late to stop him.

"What sort of book is this?" asked William. "The letters are all funny."

"It's a book written in an ancient language," said Old Isaac.

"Well, I've seen books in Latin and even one in Greek, and this doesn't look like either one to me."

"I thought you wanted to hear a story."

"Yes, from this book."

"Only from that book?"

"Yes, I want to hear the same stories that you tell Henry."

"I see," said Old Isaac, tugging at his beard, which he often did when he was thinking. "Henry, did I ever tell you about the time I was captured by pirates?"

"Pirates?!" William called out.

"It's a pity you don't want to hear that story, William. It's a good one."

"But I do! Were you really captured by pirates? When?"

~ 74 ~

"Bring over that stool, and I'll tell you."

While William went to fetch the stool, Old Isaac quickly hid away the Hebrew book that he and Henry had been reading. When they were all comfortably seated, Old Isaac began his tale.

"I was a bit younger than you two when it happened. It was right after King Ferdinand and Queen Isabella expelled me and my family from Spain."

"You must have been very naughty at school if even the Queen took notice of you," said William, visualizing the scene in his mind. He had been the subject of his schoolmaster's wrath more than once, and he was actually quite proud of some of his pranks. But he had never done anything to warrant the notice of Her Majesty Queen Elizabeth, and so he looked up at Old Isaac with a new-found respect. "Were your parents very upset?"

"No, at least I don't think so. We got separated at the port. My parents were put on one boat, and I was put on another."

Old Isaac's vision seemed to drift away, along with his thoughts, as he recalled that long-ago morning at sea. It happened in August, the hottest month of the year. He had been standing on deck, along with hundreds of other Jewish refugees, looking down at the sea, which seemed to stretch on forever and was so coolly tantalizing on such a blazing hot day, when one of the ship's mates gave the cry: "Pirates!"

The ship's captain rushed to where the mate was standing and raised his spyglass to his eye. In the distance he could see a ship, which proudly displayed its mark of identification, the dreaded symbol — the pirate flag — which was fluttering in the breeze.

"Pirates!" shouted the captain. "All hands on deck!"

In an instant, panic seized the passengers, who scrambled for a place to hide. Young Isaac scrambled, as well, but he made sure to find a hiding place where he would still be able to see the exciting battle that he knew would soon take place.

He did not have long to wait. While the crew was still hauling out their arms, the pirate ship drew near and sent over a few volleys, by way of introduction. Their cannonballs were soon followed by the pirates themselves, who stormed the ship, led by a Moorish pirate who seemed, to Young Isaac's eyes, to stand at least ten feet tall. The Spanish crew was no match for the pirates, and it wasn't long before the ship was in their hands. The seamen and the ship's captain were tied up with strong cords and thrown overboard, to the horror of the Jewish passengers, the exiles from Spain, who were unarmed and untrained in the art of war.

The Moorish pirate leader strode up and down the deck like a noble prince surveying his minions. But his face was not the benevolent face of a ruler who has the best interest of his subjects at heart. It was not a stupid or cruel face either. Instead, the pirate had the appearance of a wealthy trader surveying livestock at a county fair.

"Take only the young and healthy ones as prisoner, the ones who will fetch a good price at the slave market," the Moor commanded his followers. "Leave the rest for the sharks and the gulls."

The pirates were quick to obey their leader. They pushed the young Jewish prisoners onto the pirate ship, while the distraught parents wailed. Those who were not busy with the prisoners were involved with transferring the Spanish ship's store of fresh water and food supplies to their own ship.

Young Isaac had been watching the frantic scene with alarm. He certainly had no wish to become a slave, but without food, water and a crew to sail the Spanish ship he didn't see how those left behind could survive. He was so enwrapped in his thoughts that he didn't hear footsteps approach him from behind. He only felt himself being lifted from his hiding place when it was already too late to try to escape.

"Let's go, little one," said the Moor. "You'll make someone a fine toy."

"Please, sir, don't sell me as a slave," Young Isaac pleaded, having quickly decided that it was better to die free than live as a slave.

"And what will you give me, if I don't?" asked the pirate, amused by the boy's plea for mercy.

"I'd give you the Kingdom of Spain, if it were mine to give. But all I have is a piece of bread. It's yours, if you will let me retain my freedom."

The pirate laughed, but he took pity upon the boy, if pity is what it could be called. He dropped Young Isaac back in his hiding place, so that the other pirates wouldn't find him.

An hour later, it was all over. The pirate ship sailed away. Its cargo of Jewish slaves was never heard from again. Many of the Jews who had been left on board the Spanish ship to die did just that, since they had neither food nor water to restore their flagging spirits. But a small remnant was snatched from the eager arms of the Angel of Death when an English ship, which had seen the abandoned vessel drifting aimlessly at sea, came to their rescue.

Old Isaac was silent. It was hard to put into words the mixture of joy and fear that he had felt upon seeing that vessel. It was an odd thing, the human heart. While he had been on board the Spanish ship, a penniless refugee like the others, he had not felt lonely or afraid. But when the end of the ordeal appeared to be in sight, he suddenly realized that for him, at least, the tale was not yet over. He was a child and an orphan, with no one in the world to care about him and look after him. How would he survive this new ordeal, the ordeal of empty, unfeeling freedom?

"Is that how you came to England, Granddad?" asked Henry.

"Yes," he replied, forcing his thoughts to return to the cottage and the two boys who were waiting for him to bring his tale to an end. "Thanks to the bountiful mercies of the One Above, one of the ship's officers was … one of us. He got us all safely to London, where a few families, who were like us, were already living, and a kind-hearted family took me in." Old Isaac then turned his attention to William and said, "Well, sir, what did you think of my story?"

"I liked it very much, but there's something I don't understand. Was the Moorish pirate a good man or a bad man?"

"I suppose he was a little of both," replied Old Isaac. "Most people are."

"Were the people on the boat good people?"

"Yes, they were. They were very good people."

"Then why weren't they all saved, like you?"

Faces seemed to shimmer in the cottage's dim light, faces of his fellow passengers, faces of his father and mother, faces of the people he had known back in his town in Spain. They stretched before Old Isaac's eyes like a gauzy curtain, a tapestry of shadows that had once been full of light and animation. More and more those shadows were his companions, when he sat in the cottage, nodding over a book, waiting for Henry to arrive. And he knew that before very long he would take his place in the tableau; he would join the tapestry of souls who were past care, past hope, past life.

"Only the One Above knows the answer to that question, William," Old Isaac said slowly. It was so difficult to explain these things to a child, who saw the world in black and white and couldn't imagine that there was more to the world than what a person could see with his eyes and hear with his ears and that his own puny understanding would never puzzle the great mystery out to its end. "But we're not here to question the way the Almighty runs His world. Our task is to try to live a life that will make us worth saving."

"And you never saw your parents again?"

"No, I didn't."

William shook his head and sighed. "That's a very tragic story."

"Yes, I suppose it is."

"Have you got any comic ones?"

"I do," said Old Isaac, giving a laugh that restored him fully back to life and the present hour. "But not for today. The sun is already setting, and it's time that you and Henry were on your way home."

"Aren't you coming with us, Grandfather?" asked Henry.

"I'll be there in a bit."

When they were at the door, Old Isaac gazed down at William with a friendly eye and said, "William, now that you know our secret, about the stories, you won't tell anyone, will you?"

"Oh, no, sir! I wouldn't tell even for the Kingdom of Spain!"

ii.

William became a frequent visitor to the cottage. At first, he was content to hear Old Isaac's stories about pirates and explorers and life in London. But his curiosity had become aroused by the Hebrew books with the funny letters, which he sometimes spied sitting on the table or in a bag, before Old Isaac had a chance to put the books away. He begged the elderly man to teach him the secret code—for that is the story that Old Isaac had made up, not wishing the boy to know that the books were written in Hebrew.

Against his better judgment Old Isaac relented—William could be artfully and relentlessly persuasive when the prize was worth attaining. The boy threw himself into the study of this secret code, and by the time the cottage's thin walls trembled from the winter's blasts William could draw the letters of the Hebrew alphabet with a passable hand.

Of course, William had been sworn to secrecy about the secret code, as well. But before we judge him concerning what happened next, we must remember that he was still a child—and a child who often lived in his own imaginary world, a great stage where kings and soldiers and spies fought their battles and conquered their foes, and did it all between supper and bedtime.

The incident occurred on a day that had started out cold but fine. Sometime during the late afternoon, while William and Henry were daydreaming over their slates, talking about that future date when they would be grown and make their mark on the world, the sky turned black and icy pellets of rain came falling down. A loud clap of thunder sent Joan, who had been practicing her stitches on a bit of cloth, into a fit of ear-piercing shrieks.

Mary came rushing into the room, to comfort the little girl—for even though Joan and Henry were only her stepchildren, she had a kind heart and treated the children as though they were her own. "Hush, Joan, don't be frightened. Would you like some warm milk?"

Joan was easily convinced to go into the kitchen, since she was sure a warm piece of bread or a freshly baked bun would be offered, along with the milk. Henry went with them, to bring some refreshments for himself and his friend. While he was left alone and to his own devices, William did what he often did—he absentmindedly doodled on his slate.

There was another loud clap of thunder, and to William's surprise the front door to the Rivers home was flung open and a wild man rushed inside. He was about to call out, to alert the others to run for their lives, when on closer inspection he realized that the fearsome figure was only Henry's father, who had thrown an old blanket over his head in a vain attempt to stop the rain from drenching him to the bone.

While John Rivers was still shaking the raindrops from his clothes, he noticed that the front room of his home was empty, except for William. After asking about the whereabouts of his wife and children, and learning that they were all safely in the kitchen, John—who had changed his opinion about William after the boy's father had become an alderman of the town—greeted the child cordially. "Have you seen any cats and dogs sliding off the thatched roof?" he asked with a smile.

"No, sir," William replied. "Henry and I have been busy writing."

"Have you?" said John, moving closer to where William was sitting. "You and Henry have become quite the star scholars of Stratford, or so your father says. What are you two writing now, a poem, a history of England, another play?"

John took the slate from William's hands. In an instant, the smile was wiped from his face and replaced with a contorted expression of fierce anger.

"Where did you learn how to write these letters?" he demanded, grabbing the boy by the arm and dragging the child to his feet.

William, who had watched the change in John's face with a mixture of great interest and fear, replied, truthfully, "Let me go! You're hurting me!"

"I'll let you go, and I'll tell you to never come back. But first you'll tell me who taught you how to write Hebrew letters."

"It's not Hebrew. It's secret code."

"Did Henry's grandfather teach you these letters? Tell me!"

"I promised not to tell! Please, don't make me break my promise."

By this time Henry and Joan and Mary, and even little James, who had all heard the ruckus, had entered the room. "Mary," said John, "go back into the kitchen, and take Joan and James with you. This is between William and Henry and me."

"But you're hurting the boy."

"Go back in the kitchen, I tell you!"

James needed no further persuading. He darted back into the kitchen, where it was safe and warm. Mary reluctantly went after him, dragging behind her Joan, who had resumed her shrieking. Although Mary had learned how to smooth away her husband's sudden bursts of anger most of the time, she had also learned to respect her instincts of self-

~ 81 ~

preservation and disappear when the danger to either herself or her child, James, seemed great.

When the others had gone, John pushed Henry over to where William was standing. John then went over to the staircase and shouted, "Isaac! Isaac! Come down here! Now!"

"He's not here," said Henry, whose concern for his friend had overshadowed the fear that he normally had when his father entered into one of his rages.

"Where is he?" John demanded.

"He must have gotten caught in the storm."

Having no other vessel for his anger, John snatched the slate from William's hand and vigorously wiped it clean. After tossing it back to the boy, he said, "Go home, William. We'll finish this discussion later."

"But, Father, it's pouring outside," Henry protested. "He'll catch cold."

"He's young and healthy; he'll survive a bit of rain." John then shouted at William, "Go!"

"Yes, sir," said William, slinking toward the front door. But before he could reach it, the door was flung open a second time.

"What a storm!" called out Old Isaac. "I'm frozen to the bone. Thank the Lord there's a cheerful fire blazing in your hearth, John. It warms me just to see it."

"You want to warm yourself by the fire, do you?"

"Yes."

"In my house?"

"Yes. Is something wrong, John?" Old Isaac looked from one unhappy face to another. When he got to William's face, the boy cried out, "I didn't tell about the secret code, I promise! I didn't tell what the letters mean."

Old Isaac suddenly looked very old, as though all the life had been knocked out of him. "I believe you, William. Don't worry."

Henry wanted to lead his grandfather to the fire, because he could see that Old Isaac, who was still wearing his wet cloak, was shivering. But his father was blocking his way, and he lost his courage.

For several moments the only sound in the room was that of the rain beating its remorseless tune upon the roof. Even the fire seemed afraid to crackle and sputter. But then Old Isaac mustered whatever remained of his fading strength and said, softly, "What's my punishment to be, John? I put my white hairs at your mercy."

"If it's mercy you're after, go to your God. You'll only get justice from me."

"Oh, so you were acting according to the principles of justice when you plucked Henry and Joan from their people and raised them to be Christians. And all this time I assumed you thought you were being merciful."

"Get out of my house."

"I won't write those letters anymore," said William, who didn't understand what all the fuss was about, but was truly sorry for the role he had played in causing it. "I promise."

"Father," said Henry, "you can't turn him out on a night like this. He's an old man."

"I can and I will, and no son of mine will tell me what to do. Will you leave, Isaac, or do I have to throw you out?"

Old Isaac nodded his head several times, as though he was having a private conversation with someone, although whether that person was someone living or long gone was impossible to tell. "So it's to be banishment," he said, at last. "Well, it won't be the first time in my life."

The old man turned and opened the door. A freezing blast of wind and rain greeted him, and he drew his cloak closer to his frail body. A moment later he had disappeared into the storm.

John went over to the open door and slammed it shut. Then he remembered that William was still in the room — and that William's father could make trouble for him if the elder Shakespeare felt that his child had been mistreated by the brewer. "Henry, get a cloak for your friend. Move!"

Henry, who had watched his grandfather's departure in stunned silence, now sprang back to life. He darted up the stairs, and when he returned he had not one cloak in his hands but three. One of them he threw to William and, motioning for his friend to follow him, he raced out the door.

"Henry! Get back inside!" John called out. "Come back here!"

William managed to slip out of the room, while John was calling after his son. Between the dark and the rain, he couldn't see a thing—not Old Isaac and not his friend. And when John Rivers slammed shut the door to his house, it seemed that the last light in the world had been put out with its closing.

"Henry!" he called out. "Granddad! Where are you?"

There was no answer. He could have gone home, he knew it. But the memory of the secret he had betrayed burned within him with a scorching shame. He had to repair the damage and restore his honor. How he would do it, he didn't know. First, he had to find Henry and the old man. And so steeling himself against the merciless, blinding storm, he set off for what he hoped was the direction of the cottage.

CHAPTER VIII

Henry had raced into the storm confident that he would soon find his grandfather. His legs were young and strong, while those of Old Isaac were old and feeble, and so surely there would be no contest. He therefore was surprised to discover that his grandfather had vanished. He searched Stratford's streets, but he could see no sign of the old man anywhere.

He was glad he had thought to hide the cloak he had brought for his grandfather under the folds of his own, so that it wouldn't become soaking wet. His own cloak was already drenched and it was weighing him down, preventing him from travelling as fast as he would have liked. But even without the rain-heavy cloak, it would have been impossible to run, not when the wind was fighting against him at every step.

"Granddad!" he called out a few times. But there was no answer, except the howling wind, which seemed to mock him. Although it seemed so unlikely, Henry finally came to the conclusion that his grandfather must have decided to go to the cottage, to seek shelter there. He therefore set out in that direction.

The countryside, which seemed so gently welcoming on a pleasant summer's day, had turned treacherous. Henry's uncertain feet seemed to find every rut and puddle to fall into, and he nearly fell more times than he could count. Yet he continued, and every time there was a lull in the wind he called out, "Granddad!" and waited, in hope there would be a reply.

Whether he had gone far or not, he couldn't say; the countryside had become so wild and strange that he might have been wandering on the Steppes of Russia or the wilds of the New World for all he knew. But when he again called out, this time he thought he heard a faint reply.

"Granddad! It's Henry! Where are you?"

If there was a reply, a roar of thunder blotted it out. But the flash of lightening that followed illuminated the night scene enough for Henry to nearly jump with surprise. Just a few yards away, propped up against the trunk of an ancient tree, was Old Isaac.

"Granddad!" Henry called out again, this time with joy, as he ran with all his might.

Old Isaac, who was exhausted and freezing cold, could barely speak. "Go home, Henry," he whispered.

Henry pretended that he didn't hear. Instead, he removed the cloak he had sheltered from the storm, which was damp but better than nothing, and tried to wrap it around his grandfather's shoulders.

"You take it," said Old Isaac, trying to shake it off. "I'm an old man. I don't need it anymore."

"Don't talk nonsense," said Henry, firmly placing the cloak around Old Isaac's shivering bones. "It's cold out tonight, Granddad, and I have a cloak of my own."

Henry knew they couldn't stay beneath the tree all night. Although the old boughs provided some shelter from the rain, they didn't provide warmth. If his instincts were correct, they weren't too far from the cottage. However, he wasn't sure if his grandfather could walk even a short distance. If only he had a horse! But he didn't, and so they must try.

"We'll go to the cottage," he said, as he helped Old Isaac stand. "It will be dry there. And if there's some firewood left, we can build a fire."

"Go home, Henry," Old Isaac protested feebly. "Don't bother about me. I shall be fine."

"Come, it's not far," said Henry, again ignoring his grandfather's protests and trying to sound cheerful.

While Henry and Old Isaac were making their slow way to the cottage, William was still running wildly through the wind and rain, so lost that he despaired of ever finding his friend or his way back home.

"Henry! Granddad!" he called out, until his voice was nearly gone. "Henry!"

For his trouble, he got what felt like a bucketful of freezing rain in his face, and he fell to the ground. He had only managed to get on his knees when his eyes were blinded by a flash of lightening that seemed to reach from one end of the world to another. And he could only gape as he saw Death galloping toward him, for what else could it be riding on that powerful black beast of the night?

Somehow, William managed to shriek. Even more miraculously, the horseman heard the scream and reined in his horse in the nick of time.

"You there! What are you doing in the middle of the road?" shouted the horseman, who was trying to steer his frightened steed away from the boy.

"I have to find Henry and his Granddad."

Another flash of lightening made the nervous horse rear up on its hind legs a second time, and William struggled to hold in his own fear and not make matters worse. But something somewhere made a shrill, blood-curdling cry and the horse snorted and started and angrily pawed at the ground.

"Don't shriek, I tell you," the horseman shouted, struggling mightily to keep control of his horse, "unless you want to get trampled."

"It wasn't me," William protested. "It must be them!"

William was about to run off to find Henry and Old Isaac, when the horseman grabbed him by the back of his cloak and lifted the boy onto his saddle. "Keep your eyes open," the rider instructed William, "and tap my hand when you see your friends."

They had not ridden long when they both saw the pathetic sight, nearly at the same time. In the distance Old Isaac was lying on the ground. Henry sat beside the old man, crying.

"The storm can't last forever, Granddad," Henry was saying, trying to keep up their spirits. "Morning will come, you'll see."

He would have said more, but he thought he heard the sound of hoof beats and dared to hope that the worst really was over.

"Henry!" a familiar voice cried out. A moment later, William and the horseman were both kneeling beside Old Isaac, who painfully opened his eyes by way of greeting.

"You're here, too, William?" he whispered, trying to smile. "Can't an old man die without the whole world coming to see the show?"

"Can you walk, sir?" asked the horseman, with an air of authority.

"No, I cannot," replied Old Isaac.

"We were trying to walk a few minutes ago and he stumbled," said Henry. "I think he has sprained his ankle, or broken it."

"Are you his grandson?"

"Yes."

"Where do you live?"

"Nowhere," said Henry.

The horseman, whose stern manner had been apparent throughout the terse interview, was about to chide Henry, but William stepped forward and explained, "Granddad Isaac has been banished."

"This is no time for foolish stories," the horseman replied. "This old man needs dry clothes and a warm fire, and so do the two of you. Old man!" he said, bending low and slightly shaking the elderly man, to show that he meant business. "Tell me where you live. You ... Rabbi Isaac? What on earth are you doing here?"

Old Isaac looked into the man's face, but he didn't recognize him. The pain and wet and cold had turned everything into a blur. "You have the advantage of me, sir," he did manage to say, breathing heavily in between each word.

"I'm Dr. Lopez. Rodrigo Lopez. From London. Surely you remember me."

"This is a miracle."

"But we don't rely on miracles. You must tell me where you live. You must get yourself warm."

"My grandson spoke the truth. I no longer have a home."

"He was banished for teaching me ..."

Old Isaac, who still had enough wits about him to remember that William was listening, made a motion to Henry to be silent. To Dr. Lopez, he said, "You were acquainted with my son-in-law, if I recall. I wanted to instruct Henry, his son, in certain matters, and now I can't go back to their home."

"I see. But we have to find a place where you can spend the night."

"There's a cottage not too far from here," said Henry. "That's where we were headed, when my grandfather fell."

"Then it will have to do," said Dr. Lopez, as he helped Old Isaac stand up.

ii.

If the first miracle that night had been the appearance of Dr. Lopez, the second was the existence of a good supply of firewood inside the cottage. Once Old Isaac was settled as comfortably as was possible on the rickety bed, Dr. Lopez got a good blaze going in the hearth. The two boys gratefully gravitated to its warmth, and their happiness would have been complete if there also had been some food and drink. But the only refreshments in the cottage were the medicines in Dr. Lopez's bag, and that was not for them.

Instead, Dr. Lopez was trying to coax his patient, Old Isaac, to take a swallow of some brew. But after the elderly man took a sip, he coughed most of it out.

"That's a bitter way to spend my final moments in this world," said Old Isaac, pushing away the bottle. "No more."

"I'm trying to save your life."

"Don't waste your powders. It's too late for me."

"It's forbidden to give up hope. There has to be a reason why I was on that road this night. If it wasn't to save your life, why was I detained at an earl's house, which made me set out late for London and get caught in this storm?"

"I know nothing about princes and earls. But I do know that it wasn't on my account that you got a drenching. If you were meant to save someone's life, it must be Henry."

"Your grandson?" Dr. Lopez looked over to the fireplace, where the two boys were sitting. He was certain there was nothing wrong with either one of them that a good night's sleep and a hearty breakfast in the morning wouldn't cure.

"Take him to London with you," Old Isaac pleaded, suddenly very serious. "Find him a nice girl to marry; someone from one of our families."

"Are you certain that this is what he wants?"

"Henry!" Old Isaac called out, with what remained of his fading strength.

Henry left his seat by the fire and approached the bed. "Yes, Grandfather?"

"Dr. Lopez will take you with him to London, if you agree. He will find you a home, among our people. It would make me very happy if you would go. But the decision is up to you."

"Who will take care of you, if I leave Stratford?"

When his grandfather didn't reply, Henry looked to Dr. Lopez for an answer. When that gentleman was also silent, Henry said, "I'll go to London, Granddad."

Old Isaac tried to lift his arm, but he was too weak. "Dr. Lopez, there is a ring on my finger," he said. "Could you please remove it for me?" When the ring was sitting in the palm of Old Isaac's hand, he said to Henry, "Your great-grandmother gave me this ring, before we were married. That was a long time ago. Now I want you to have it. But, Henry, London is a big city and there are many temptations. Promise me that you'll never sell this ring. Promise me that."

"I won't sell it. Granddad ..." Henry knew in his heart what he wanted to say, but the words were all choked and tangled.

"I know, Henry, I know. There's no need for words."

Henry reluctantly took the ring and turned away from the bed, so that his grandfather could not see his tears. He went to sit in a corner, whose dark shadows were strangely comforting to his troubled heart.

Dr. Lopez was trying to convince Old Isaac to take another sip of the medicine when William, who had been watching the entire scene from a discrete distance, came forward and said, "Dr. Lopez, may I have a word with Granddad Isaac, in private?"

"If he is feeling up to it. Rabbi Isaac, have you strength to speak with this young man?"

Old Isaac nodded his head, and Dr. Lopez retired to a seat by the fire.

"Well, William?"

"Granddad Isaac, is the Angel of Death in the room?" asked William, keeping one eye on the old man and the other on the cottage's nooks and crannies, in case that awesome being should make its appearance while he was busy speaking to Old Isaac.

"Yes, he is."

"Then you're really going to die?"

"Yes, I am."

"Have you anything to give me?"

"I'm sorry, William, but I fear that another injustice is about to be done. It's true that you've been like another grandson to me, but I seem to be leaving the world without many material possessions."

"You don't have another ring?"

~ 91 ~

"No, but let me think. I know what I can give you. I shall give you my stories."

"Your stories?"

"Yes, they're yours now. Will you promise that you'll take good care of them?"

"I will. And I'll tell the world about what Henry's father did to you, how mean he was, and cruel."

"No, William, don't do that. I know you're still very young, but try to remember that most people are ... well, human beings. They may not always behave as we would wish, but often it's when they hurt us the most that they are most in need of our compassion. Now, please tell Dr. Lopez that I'd like to speak with him again."

When Dr. Lopez had returned to his side, Old Isaac asked the physician to help him say the *Vidui*, the Jew's final confession. But before they began the prayer, Old Isaac remembered that there was still one more thing that needed to be taken care of.

"You'll see that I'll get a proper burial, won't you? I wouldn't be able to die in peace, if I thought there would be a cross hanging over my head after I'm gone."

"I'll take care of it," Dr. Lopez assured him.

"And dig the grave in some secluded spot, somewhere where no one will find my grave and dig up my bones and throw them all about. I want to have all of them with me when it's time for the End of Days and the Resurrection."

"I'll do my best."

"Thank you. Now I'm ready. There's a prayer book in that bag over there."

Dr. Lopez removed the prayer book from the bag that Old Isaac always carried with him. The physician was not a man who prayed often, and so it took him a few minutes to find the correct page. Old Isaac's eyes were already closed and his face was a ghostly ashen color, when Dr. Lopez said the first words.

"*Ashamnu,* we have sinned ..."

"*Ashamnu.*"

"Bagadnu, we have betrayed ..."
"Bagadnu ..."

iii.

The next morning was gray and cold but at least it had stopped raining. Henry helped Dr. Lopez dig Old Isaac's grave, while William kept a lookout, to make sure they were not disturbed in their sorry task. The rain-sodden earth was difficult to shovel, and the two gravediggers had to stop to rest several times. When at last Old Isaac had been laid in his final resting place, Henry asked if they should say anything.

"We don't have ten men here," Dr. Lopez explained. "You can say the *Kaddish* prayer when you get to London. But you can place a stone on the grave. It's one of our customs."

Henry found a stone, and did as Dr. Lopez instructed. William also put a stone on the grave, now that his job as watchman was done.

Dr. Lopez went to untie his horse. He had not expected to be detained overnight, and he was anxious to get to London without further delay.

Henry felt torn between the wish to stay beside the grave of his grandfather and hold on to the bond between them, and the desire to begin this new chapter in his young life. After a brief struggle, youth won out.

"Goodbye, William," he said.

"Goodbye? Where are you going?"

"To London. I'm going with Dr. Lopez."

"Why? Are you sick?"

"No, I'm not sick."

"What shall I tell your father? He's sure to ask."

"Tell him ... tell him I've gone home."

Henry climbed onto the saddle, behind Dr. Lopez, and the two rode off. William followed them with his eyes, until the horse and riders disappeared down the great highway that led to London.

LONDON

CHAPTER IX

At first, William dearly missed his childhood friend and the many happy hours he had spent with Henry and Old Isaac in the cottage. But it is the way of the world for people to be busy. As he grew and matured to be a young man, William, too, became busy with other things. Some say that during these years he was a poacher or a butcher or a teacher. It's also said that he loved one girl, but married another. What is known is that he married in 1582, to a woman named Anne Hathaway. Two years later, the Catholic head of the Arden family, Edward Arden—who was related to William's mother, Mary Arden—was arrested for plotting to murder the Protestant Queen Elizabeth. Although many people thought he was innocent, Edward Arden was executed.

It was around this time that William Shakespeare disappeared from recorded history. When he next turned up, he was already a rising star in the firmament of London's glittering theatre world.

We will pass over the very early plays. A writer must start somewhere, and it is better to begin a career with a play like *Titus Andronicus* than to spend a lifetime writing plays and end up with nothing better. And since we know practically nothing about William's activities during those first years in London—we shall not waste pen and ink on refuting the claim that he was wont to hold horses outside London's theatres and that is how he got his start—we shall resume our acquaintanceship during that remarkable time when his play *Romeo and Juliet* was the most talked about play in town.

The play was discussed and admired not only in the great houses that lined the Thames, but also in more modest abodes. But perhaps nowhere was it "drawn and quartered" with such sharp critical knives as at a certain public house that was frequented by both personages from the theatre and those who merely loved to see a play and talk about it afterward for hours.

On one such afternoon, the ale house was packed with a rowdy crowd that was quenching their thirst—for play-going was a thirsty business, as everyone knew—with the owner's hearty brew.

"And I say it could be done," said an occupant of one of the long wooden benches, who from his dress and calloused hands appeared to be a joiner.

"And I say it couldn't," said his companion, who owned a cobbling establishment in town.

"My Granddad used to speak about a potion that could make a person sleep like a corpse for three nights. Or did it keep a person awake?" The glover could be counted upon to never get his facts straight, as his friends knew very well. Fortunately for him, though, his gloves were of a better quality than his memory.

"I still say there's no such thing," said the cobbler, who insisted on veracity in plays. "Either a person's dead, or he isn't."

The blacksmith, a heavy-set man who had been listening to the lively conversation in his own ponderous way, shook his head and lamented, "That's the trouble with these new plays. The children are always rebelling against their parents' wishes. If that Romeo and Julianne had been my children ..."

"Juliet," said the joiner.

"What?"

"The girl's name is Juliet, and I thought the boy who played her was remarkable—so lady-like and refined."

The owner of the ale house had come over to the table with a fresh round of drinks. Having overheard the last comment, he added a quip of his own. "And where did you learn about refined manners, Thomas? From your hammer or your nails?"

Everyone laughed, because they were in the mood to hold on to the pleasures of the day for as long as they could; there would be time enough to return to the daily grind. The ale house owner wished the group good health, and moved on to the next table.

The joiner, who thought himself something of an expert on the London theatre, despite his lowly profession, fortified himself with a long drink of ale before divulging what he considered to be the final word on their afternoon's entertainment. "I say that *Romeo and Juliet* is the best play that William Shakespeare has written yet. Mark my words, he's one to watch."

Those final words were overheard by a morose-looking middle-aged man who was seated at a place at the next table. In truth, he had several places at that table all too himself, because the wooden surface was covered with dozens of heavily marked manuscript pages. An inkwell was also sitting on the table, and its companion, a quill pen, was sitting in the hand of the owner of all this stuff, Henry Chettle, playwright. "Shakespeare. Shakespeare," he muttered to himself, while taking a break from composing some dialogue for his new play. "Is there no other topic in town except William Shakespeare?"

"Calm yourself, Mr. Chettle," said the ale house owner, who was searching for an unoccupied place on the table to place Mr. Chettle's tankard of beer. "You know how it is when a new play opens, being a man of the theatre yourself."

"If you can call his rants and ravings theatre," quipped the joiner, in a stage whisper that could be heard halfway across the room.

"What's that? What did you say?" Mr. Chettle rose magnificently to take the bait and his performance was marred only by the fact that he wasn't sure who had spoken.

He therefore jerked his body from side to side in a manner that bordered on the ridiculous.

"Careful, Mr. Chettle, or you'll spill your ink," said the ale house owner, who didn't mind a little tomfoolery in his tavern, but drew the line — with his strong fists, if he had to — at a brawl.

"You mark *my* words, you ... you ... pit dwellers," said Mr. Chettle, addressing his remarks in a general way to the occupants of the next table. "The works of Henry Chettle will live on long after that precious peacock of yours is forgotten."

"Is that so?" said the joiner, who had also risen from his place. "I suppose you'd have the courage to say that to Mr. Shakespeare's face?"

"I'd welcome the opportunity."

"Well, if I'm not mistaken," said the joiner, "here's your chance."

The door to the ale house had swung open. Standing in the doorway, like three young gods who had graciously deigned to step down from their airy pedestals for the afternoon, were the current three idols of the London stage. To the right stood the actor Richard Burbage, who in the triumphal role of Romeo had conquered even the coldest and most mildewed of hearts. To the left stood the comedian William Kempe, who had made the theatre roar with laughter at his star turn in the minor part of Peter, for it was his way to steal the show, regardless the size of the role. In the center stood the creator of all that poetry and madness, the playwright William Shakespeare, who had long since disposed of any country-bumpkin mannerisms he might have possessed and was now very much a man of the town.

When the occupants of the ale house realized who had just made their entrance, they all began to whistle and cheer. It was for moments like this that they came to this tavern, where the prices were high but the possibility of having a brush with genius made a visit worthwhile.

The three young men acknowledged the applause, and then they made their way to their table, which the ale house owner always kept in reserve for members of the Lord Chamberlain's Men.

On their way they passed the table where Henry Chettle was sitting and Richard Burbage, who was as much astute businessman as acclaimed actor, wished the playwright a good afternoon. Mr. Chettle acknowledged the greeting and stiffly bowed to William Kempe, while pointedly ignoring Shakespeare.

"Is that a new play you are writing?" asked Richard, letting his eye fall upon the mess of papers.

"It is."

Richard picked out the title page and read, "*The Tragedy of Hoffmann, Prince of Weimar*. It sounds thrilling. When does it open?"

"The same day it closes, judging by the success of his other plays," said William Kempe, who lacked the diplomatic touch.

The crowd laughed uproariously; Kempe was such a favorite that it hardly mattered what he said. People started laughing even before he finished his sentence, and so even if the quip turned out to be disappointing it was already too late to stop.

Yet it was not at Kempe that the playwright Chettle was glaring at with an open display of anger and hate. "You ... you ..." he sputtered at William Shakespeare, who was regarding the older playwright with a carefully honed half-smirk that managed to look both sweet and insolent at the same time.

Mr. Chettle, to his dismay and disappointment, could think of no way to end his speech in triumph. He therefore gathered up his manuscript and stormed out of the ale house, trying to hide his humiliation behind a cloak of righteous indignation.

The ale house owner led his three stars to their table, where he noticed that a stool was missing. "I shall bring one at once," he assured the young men, but Kempe stopped him.

"There's no need. I've already got one."

Kempe then grabbed a stool out from under a man who was drinking with his friends at the next table. The man fell to the floor, and the crowd laughed their appreciation at the prank. The man rose to his feet and his angry face showed that he wasn't about to let anyone get away with treating him in such an ignoble fashion. But before he could curl his fat fingers into a fist he saw who his opponent was and his anger turned to delight. This was a story that he could bore his family and friends with for a lifetime—the fabled time he had been at the butt of a joke perpetrated by the most famous comic actor in England, Will Kempe.

"Really, Kempe, was that necessary?" drawled Richard, after the comedian had joined them at the table. "If you don't learn how to behave, we won't be able to take you with us when we perform before the Queen."

Kempe stretched out his legs and surveyed the crowded room with satisfaction. "It's good to be young and famous. Now, if I only had a drink."

In an instant he was on his feet—in truth, he never sat still for more than a few moments—and was prowling about the room. When he spied his next dupe he approached the unsuspecting man from behind and with one quick, flawless movement deftly separated the man from his tankard of ale. The comedian made his escape from the "scene of the crime" by leaping on top of a table and merrily jigging his way across the other tabletops to the place where Burbage and Shakespeare were sitting.

The crowd roared—but does anyone still need to be told that?

This time Kempe remained seated; he had a full tankard of beer in his hand and he drank it with pleasure.

"You should take our Kempe as an example," Richard said to William, who was studying a page that listed the cash receipts from the week's performances. "Life isn't only about money and work. You need to learn how to enjoy life."

William glanced over at the clown, who was savoring his drink with the delight of a child tasting a lump of sugar for the first time. "Life is easy when everything is a joke."

At the mention of the word "joke," Kempe snapped open his eyes, put down his ale, somersaulted onto the table and crouched on his haunches before William and Richard. "Speaking of jokes, I have an idea for our next play."

"Would you get off the table," said William, who appreciated the clown's beneficial effect upon ticket sales, but found Kempe's nonstop antics offstage to be too much.

Kempe obliged by doing a back flip, which landed him once more onto his stool. Without pausing to take a breath, he continued, "The play starts off with two young gallants who have to leave town."

"Why?" asked William.

"How should I know why? You're the playwright."

"Thank you for remembering."

"You're welcome. Now where was I?"

"Padua? Mantua?" Richard asked, languidly. Italian settings for plays were a running joke with his theatre company. But what could they do? The audience loved the plays, and so who were they to disappoint them?

"No!" said Kempe. "Verona!"

"*Romeo and Juliet* is set in Verona," said William, "as you may recall."

"No matter," said Kempe. "We'll use the same sets. It will save the company money."

"My father will like that," said Richard, whose father, James Burbage, was the company's business manager and the man who had built their playhouse, The Theatre. "Go on, Kempe. What happens next?"

"So, the two gentlemen are in Verona, and they fall in love, and the lovers get all mixed up, and then everything gets straightened out. The end."

"How?" asked William.

"How what?"

"How do the lovers get mixed up? How does everything get straightened out?"

"How do I know how?"

"You're the playwright, William," said Richard.

"Thank you for remembering."

"Why the resistance?" asked Kempe. "It's a fantastic idea. It will be the hit of the season."

"You mean it *was* the hit of the season," said William. "We already did that play. It was called *The Comedy of Errors*, remember?"

"Where's my mind? Where's my mind? That's what comes from using it too much. The poor thing's already worn out. I forgot to mention the most important part."

"Yours?" asked Richard.

"Of course, there will be a part for William Kempe. Your name may be in the play's title, Romeo, but I'm the one that the people pay to see."

"Really?" said Richard, who had too much self-confidence (some might call it conceit), to be offended by the company clown's jibes. Indeed, unlike Shakespeare, he liked to encourage the clown to ramble, because often there was something of use hidden amongst all the nonsense.

"You've got to give the dogs a bone, if you want to succeed in the theatre," said Kempe, warming to his subject. "I always say: The Muses are for poets. A player's fortune is in the pit."

"The fool turns philosopher," Richard said to William.

"But what a philosophy!"

"And while I'm on the subject of playwriting," Kempe continued, "William, you're a nice young man, and you've got talent, but let me give you some advice. Not so many words, this time. Not so many words."

William stared at the clown, not yet deciding if this so-called advice was worthy of a reply or if a haughty silence was the best answer. To his surprise, Richard turned to him and said, "The fool has a point. You have me lying dead in that tomb for an eternity."

"That's what I'm saying," said Kempe. "It's not natural for a person to be dead for so long."

William finished off his drink and replaced it on the table with a punctuating thud. "Thank you both for your most constructive criticism. In the future, I shall try to restrain my pen."

"Then we're agreed?" asked Kempe.

"About what?"

"Our next play."

"Kempe," said Richard, waving his hand to get the clown's attention. "Oh, Kempe, you haven't yet told us how your new idea is different from the old play."

"If the two of you would let me speak without getting me off the subject a thousand times, I'd tell you." He waited a few moments, for dramatic effect. "It's the girl."

"What girl?" William asked.

"What does it matter, what girl?" Kempe snapped. "The point is that she has to dress up like a man."

"So?"

"William!!! You'll drive me mad!!!"

Richard, who was sitting in between the two warring parties, held out his hands to silence them both. "Wait. Wait. Wait a minute. Kempe, are you saying that a boy actor who is pretending to be a woman has to then pretend to be a man?"

"The audience will love it!" Kempe exclaimed, returning to his formerly happy self, already hearing the roars of laughter.

"I think he's on to something, William. That's never been done before."

"It might have potential," William reluctantly conceded.

"Might?!" Kempe exploded. "I'm handing you the greatest idea for a story since Eve handed Adam the apple, and you're telling me it might have potential?"

"But why does the girl have to dress up like a man?"

Kempe threw up his hands in disgust. "Oh, William, I don't know." He then made a gesture to throttle the young man. "You're the playwright!"

ii.

Time passed and, as the saying goes, all good things must come to an end. James Burbage was standing outside his theatre directing a workman, who was affixing a sign over an older one, whose faded letters read:

FINAL PERFORMANCES!
THE TRAGEDY OF ROMEO AND JULIET

"It's not straight," said James Burbage. "A little higher on the right side."

The workman obliged, inching the sign a little higher, until Burbage shouted out, "There!"

When the worker had finished affixing the sign to the wall, he moved aside. Burbage surveyed with satisfaction the new sign, which read:

OPENING NEXT WEEK!
A NEW COMEDY
THE TWO GENTLEMEN OF VERONA

William, who had come out into the street, went over to James Burbage and took a look at the new sign, as well.

"How did the rehearsal go?" asked Burbage.

"Well enough. We'll be ready to open."

"I'm sure it will be a success, William, but to be honest, I'll be sorry to see Romeo and Juliet go. They were a very profitable pair for The Theatre. But maybe we can revive them in the summer."

"Have the censors approved the new play?"

~ 104 ~

"Not yet. But don't worry. There's never anything in your plays to give the censors offense."

Their conversation was interrupted by the noise of a rowdy crowd that had appeared in the street, seemingly out of nowhere. The crowd's attention, as well as their jeers, was focused on a horse-drawn enclosed wagon, the kind used to haul prisoners to the Tower. The wagon was occupied and the prisoner's face could be seen anxiously peering through the small window cut into the back of the wagon's high wall. The man's large dark eyes and black hair suggested that he was a foreigner. The taunts of the crowd, who were yelling "Tinoco to the Tower," supplied the rest of the information. Everyone in London had heard of Senor Tinoco by this time, even William. For even though he had a new play that was about to open and, as usual, he had immersed himself in rehearsals and rewrites, to the exclusion of just about anything else, news of the latest plot to assassinate the Queen had been too sensational for even him to ignore.

The constable accompanying the wagon was trying to clear the street, so that the prisoner could be conveyed to his cell. But it was no easy task, because in addition to the jeerers there was the usual assortment of carters and laborers clogging the narrow street.

"Another one of them spies going to the Tower," said James Burbage, nodding toward the wagon. "I want this to be the subject of your next play."

"The Tower?"

"Of course not—I'm talking about the Spanish plot to poison the Queen."

"Oh, that."

James Burbage turned to his most promising playwright and stared. If he had been in the ale house on that afternoon a few months earlier, he would have agreed with Kempe's assessment of Shakespeare: He liked William, and he thought William had talent. But he sometimes wondered about Shakespeare's business sense. The young man was ambitious—he seemed to like the things that money and fame could buy—but he was still an idealist; he wanted to raise the level of the theatre and he therefore eschewed the sensationalist subjects and stale tricks that had been the stock and trade of an earlier generation. But there was a time and a place for everything, in Burbage's opinion, and he was sorry that Shakespeare was no Christopher Marlowe, who had never missed an opportunity to capitalize on the latest sensation.

But Marlowe was dead and Shakespeare was alive, and Burbage was a pragmatic business man. He therefore patiently tried to explain his point. "William, this is the biggest scandal to hit London since that Mary of Scotland was executed. Imagine—and you're a talented playwright and so you, more than anyone, should be able to see the dramatic potential in the story—imagine the situation: Our Queen's own physician, who holds her precious life in his two hands, has been employed by the Catholic King of Spain to kill her. All that devil of a doctor Lopez had to do was put a little poison in her sleeping powder, and poor Elizabeth would never have woken up. It's a good thing the Earl of Essex got wind of the plot in time."

"Yes, Essex is always up to something," William replied. He hadn't told his theatre associates about his Catholic relatives in the countryside; he hadn't even told them that he was married and the father of several children. Catholics weren't popular in the circles he was now traveling in, and so he thought it best to let sleeping dogs lie. Yet even though he had no problem with conforming to the currently popular Protestant dogma, it irked him—the open hostility, the disparaging remarks—which had become engrained in the public discourse. Even cultured people, men who could speak with compassion about the noble savages of Africa and the New World, thought any speech, even the vilest, was permissible when it came to the Catholics. He therefore added, expressing his bitterness more openly than usual, "Perhaps Essex amuses the Queen with his exploits, but in my opinion there's already been more than enough enmity

~ 106 ~

stirred up between Protestants and Catholics. I should think the English public would be bored with these intrigues by now."

"Bored? With hating Catholics?" Burbage scratched his head. Yes, there were definitely times when he wished it was Marlowe who was writing for the Lord Chamberlain's Men, and it was a pity that the man had died so young.

"But I don't want a play about Catholics," Burbage clarified. "I want a play about a Jew. It's that Jew Lopez that's got everyone all riled up. William, are you listening to me?"

Burbage watched with exasperation as William darted into the street to retrieve a small gray monkey, which had somehow escaped from its cage during the tumult surrounding the prisoner caged in the wagon.

"Yes, I'm listening, Mr. Burbage," said William, when he returned, although his attention was really fastened upon the tiny monkey, who seemed as fascinated by William as William was with him.

"This is serious, William. I wouldn't be surprised if Henslowe decides to pull *The Jew of Malta* out of the mothballs to capitalize on this scandal. But we'll beat him at his game. We'll put on our own play about a Jew. William! Are you listening to me?"

"I'm doing research for the new play," said William. "Tell me, Senor Monkey, everything you know about this Spanish plot. If you don't confess, I'll put you on the rack and torture you until you do."

"Hush, William," said Burbage. "I don't know what's gotten into you today. Never make jokes about what goes on in the Tower. You never know who might be listening."

"That's right."

William and James Burbage froze. They did not yet know who had spoken those two words, for the person was standing behind them, but the assurance with which the words were said, along with the subtly mocking tone, made them both painfully aware that the speaker was obviously a person that it would have been better not to have offended.

"You give your playwright sound advice, Mr. Burbage," the voice continued.

The two slowly turned—it would be unpardonably rude to make the personage come round to them. Standing before them, in all his vigorous and vain glory, was Robert Devereux, the 2nd Earl of Essex.

"My lord, what an unexpected ..." James Burbage, who was seldom at a loss for words, was at a loss for them now. Not only was the Earl of Essex the current favorite of the Queen, but he had recently been appointed a member of the Privy Council, where he could indulge his love of political intrigue to his heart's content. Since his heart was rarely content, for his political ambitions were immense, he was a man to be first avoided, and, when that wasn't possible, flattered and feared.

"Pleasure, I hope?" responded Essex, helpfully supplying the missing word.

"A pleasure and an honor, my lord."

"And for that honor I have a favor to ask of you in return. I believe I stand in the presence of William Shakespeare, do I not?"

"Yes, my lord."

"Please introduce him to me."

"Of course, my lord," said Burbage bowing low, and he would have bowed even lower except that the tip of his hat was already touching the ground. "My lord of Essex, William Shakespeare. William, may I present to you Robert Devereux, Earl of Essex, valiant hero of the battlefield, distinguished member of the Privy Council, who may one day, if England is so privileged, serve our country as her next Secretary of State, and who, as a generous patron of the arts and letters, holds the future of our small and lowly theatre in his most high, exalted and gracious hands."

Essex smiled, while Shakespeare bowed and murmured, "My lord."

"You are a most fortunate man, Mr. Shakespeare," said Essex. "Your comedies have found favor in the eyes of our sovereign."

"You honor me too much, my lord."

"I wonder if I should tell the Queen your little joke about the way I interrogate her prisoners. She does so love to laugh."

"Oh, my lord," protested Burbage, "such a poor, trifling jest is hardly worthy of your attention, or Her Majesty's. I hope."

"I defer to your superior wisdom in this matter," said Essex. "But, Mr. Shakespeare, for your information, stranger creatures than this monkey have been known to betray a queen. Good day."

William and Burbage bowed as the Earl of Essex, followed by his retinue, made their way back to their horses, which were standing not far from the wagon conveying the prisoner, which was still stalled in the street.

"I trust you will be comfortable in your new quarters in the Tower, Senor Tinoco," Essex cheerfully called out to the prisoner, and then he rode off.

A few moments later the already confused scene received angry reinforcements from a new mob that swooped down upon the prisoner's wagon.

"Traitor! Murderer! Dirty foreigner!" they shouted, while shaking their fists. "Go back to where you came from!"

When a few of them began to throw rocks at the wagon, which was government property, the constable woke up. "You there, what do you think you're doing? Don't harm the wagon. Driver, get going! Go!"

The wagon rumbled off, followed by the mob, which was still yelling and screaming at the top of their lungs. William wondered, as he watched their energetic performance, if the outburst had been truly spontaneous or if they had been hired by someone—perhaps the Earl of Essex himself, since he was the one who was at the head of the investigation into the assassination plot.

James Burbage had been watching the scene, as well. "You don't want the Earl of Essex to not like you, William. Maybe you should dedicate your next book of poems to him to make amends."

The monkey, which William was still holding, clapped its hands and smiled. For a moment, William thought the animal was showing his approval of Burbage's suggestion. Then he noticed that one of the cart drivers was approaching them.

"Please, sir, my monkey," said the man, with an accent that showed he was not English-born and bred.

William handed over the monkey, which waved as its owner carried it away.

CHAPTER X

Although the Earl of Essex was a savvy enough courtier to never appear unduly ruffled in public, unless putting on a sulky show could serve his purpose, the remark he had heard outside The Theatre had displeased him. If people were joking about him in the streets of London today, they would be sniggering in the palace hallways tomorrow—and the Queen seldom backed a loser, no matter how pretty his head and no matter how much he amused her.

All this he was thinking and more, as he prepared to take part in the day's jousting tournament, for if there was anything that all England loved more than the theatre, it was a tournament. On the field a young man could make his mark, further rise in the Queen's opinion, or lose everything, and Essex knew what he had to accomplish on this day. He had to prove on the tournament field that he was the young, vigorous hope of England; his sun must permanently eclipse the waning moon of old, doddering William Cecil—the country's former Secretary of State, present Lord Treasurer, and the Queen's most trusted advisor—as well as dim the rising star of Cecil's contemptible son, Robert, who had never had to set a single dainty toe on the battlefield, since he had a father to fight all his battles for him.

It wasn't supposed to have turned out this way. A tournament was usually just an amusement for someone like Essex, not an event where a reputation was at stake. But things had not been going well in his bid to be England's next Secretary of State.

It was the fault of those slippery Portuguese, he thought to himself angrily, as his servant encased him in his armor. His spies had captured a few of them, such as Esteban Ferreira da Gama, a Portuguese gentleman who was supposedly a loyal follower of Don Antonio, the Pretender to the Portuguese throne who had received the backing of the English monarch, Elizabeth; Ferreira was suspected of being a double agent for the King of Spain, like most of the Portuguese spies. At the other end of the social spectrum was Gomez d'Avila, a Portuguese nobody currently living in Holborn, who had been arrested while disembarking from a ship in Sandwich; the charge was that he was carrying a suspicious letter, which he must have been given in Flanders, the country of origin of the vessel.

"The bearer will inform your Worship in what price your pearls are held. I will advise your Worship presently of the utmost penny that can be given for them."

Essex could quote the translated text of the letter by heart. In addition to the price of the pearls, there was a discussion about the price of musk and amber, and whether or not the letter's intended recipient, whose name wasn't stated, wished to be a partner in the enterprise. It was all a code, of course, a secret code. But what the devil did it mean?

He had intercepted other letters, including letters sent from Ferreira to the Queen's physician, Dr. Lopez—a man who was also on Essex's list of people to despise, since the physician had once made a jest at court at Essex's expense. Another letter, this one from Dr. Lopez to Ferreira, was also in Essex's possession. Ferreira had warned the physician that he must prevent, at all costs, the arrival of d'Avila in England. The physician had replied that he had already written to Brussels several times and would spare no expense, even if it cost him £300.

Essex wasn't sure how much Lopez had paid, but that part of the plot had failed. D'Avila had arrived on English shores, where he had been promptly arrested. That had all gone well. After Ferreira had been questioned and d'Avila had been shown the rack, they had both confessed. The gentlemanly Ferreira had suavely pointed a finger at Dr. Lopez, claiming that the physician was in the pay of King Philip of Spain and at the center of the plot to poison Don Antonio, the Portuguese Pretender. The low class d'Avila had admitted, with shaking lips and wild gestures, to being a courier between Ferreira and another Portuguese agent, this one named Tinoco, who was stationed in Brussels and was an agent of the King of Spain. The letters that d'Avila carried also had been about a plot to get rid of Don Antonio.

Tinoco had been arrested at Dover—the web Essex had spun was efficient, he thought with grim satisfaction. The courier had denied everything, at first, as was only natural. He had insisted that he had come to England to warn the Queen about a Jesuit plot against her life. But if the man thought that Robert Devereux, England's future Secretary of State, was going to accept a feeble story like that, the Portuguese prisoner was sadly mistaken. He had managed to pry out of the man a story that was more to his liking: Tinoco confessed that he had been sent to England by the Spanish king. His mission was to convince Dr. Lopez to do a service for King Philip of Spain. Ferreira was to have assisted Tinoco in his task of persuading Lopez.

It should have been smooth sailing from there, Essex thought angrily, as he moved his arms to ensure that the armor had been secured correctly. But he had achieved too little too late. The Queen had lost interest in trying to place Don Antonio, who was nothing more than a spoiled weakling, on the Portuguese throne. Furthermore, Antonio's presence in England, where he held court in a lavish style at Eton, had become a burden upon the English treasury. It was common knowledge that the Queen wouldn't mind it at all if someone were to assassinate Don Antonio, and thereby remove the problem of the Portuguese Pretender's existence—and expense account. Of course, nothing was ever said outright. It was all insinuated by vague hints and sighs.

Essex had been at court long enough to know how to interpret those hints; he therefore knew that were he to now reveal that he had thwarted a plot to assassinate the Portuguese Pretender, he would gain nothing but the Queen's displeasure and the scorn of the Cecils. Yes, life had been very unkind to the Earl, and he felt the sting of shame to his very marrow. All his hard work during the past several months had come to nothing. The Cecils were probably now with the Queen in her Royal Pavilion, laughing at his incompetence.

That thought was still in his mind when the flap to his own pavilion was raised and his assistant and personal spy master, Anthony Bacon, entered. After Essex's servant removed himself from the tent, Essex cast an angry glance at the courtier and said, "Well?"

"Tinoco insists he knows nothing more."

"You showed him the rack?"

"We did as you commanded, my lord," Bacon replied, like the crafty politician that he was.

"You showed him the other letter, the one about the pearls and amber and musk? It must be referring to more than one plot."

"He insists that he knows nothing about the letter's contents or how to break the code."

"You do realize, Mr. Bacon, that your gaggle of no-nothing Portuguese geese is turning me into a laughingstock at court?"

"Unraveling assassination plots takes time, my lord. With your permission, we will continue our interrogation of the prisoners and continue to watch the ports and intercept all correspondence from Spanish and Portuguese agents before it enters England. We will find the letter incriminating Dr. Lopez. I promise. "

"Don't waste my time and money finding more proof that Lopez is involved in the plot against Don Antonio. We must prove something much grander. We must prove that he is the instigator of a plot to poison the Queen. That is the incriminating letter you must find."

"If the letter exists, we will find it, my lord."

"And if it doesn't exist?"

Anthony Bacon smiled. "Letters have a way of turning up."

"Then make sure it does, and that it turns up soon. You promised me that this Spanish plot would make my career. Break that promise, and I'll break you."

"Yes, my lord."

ii.

It was a glorious day for a tournament. Those who had not been lucky enough to get a view of the lists, where the contests would be fought, contented themselves with other amusements. While colorful banners fluttered overhead in the breeze, a troupe of traveling entertainers — musicians and jugglers and tumblers — amused the common folk, who were picnicking on the grounds.

The lists themselves were partially surrounded by gaily patterned pavilions. The largest and most elegant was the pavilion that belonged to Queen Elizabeth, who was entertaining the Cecils and other high-ranking government officials in her royal tent, as the Earl of Essex had supposed.

In another pavilion was the "Essex Circle," as that group was commonly known. The wife of the Earl of Essex, Frances Walsingham, who was the daughter of the deceased spy master, Francis Walsingham, played hostess to a glittering crowd of courtiers and literati — luminaries such as Henry Wriothesley, the Earl of Southampton, and Edward de Vere, the Earl of Oxford, who were the very cream of the intellectually and artistically inclined nobility.

A sound of trumpets summoned the spectators to turn their attention from their droll conversations and the tables laden with food and drink to the field, which had been prepared for the next joust.

Essex had already emerged from his pavilion and mounted his steed. One of his pages handed him his helmet, and then another one handed him his lance. Thus accoutered, he rode onto the field.

His opponent met him at the center of the field. The two turned to salute the Queen, and then they took their places at opposite ends of the list.

The trumpets sounded again, and at the signal the two horsemen rushed forward, urging their horses to gallop, race, fly with all their might. The two lances met and struck their blows. Essex lost his balance and fell from his horse.

The crowd gasped. In the ensuing moments there was a sustained murmur as they waited, almost as one, to see if the blow had been fatal or not. The murmur grew louder as Essex began to show signs of life. After a few minutes, he rose to his knees and removed his helmet, to breath in some fresh air unimpeded. Meanwhile, one of his pages had arrived on the scene and he helped his master to his feet.

Essex tried his limbs, which were sore from the fall but not broken. He then turned his gaze to the pavilion where his wife and friends were seated. They were merrily chatting and drinking from their cups of wine. If his fall had alarmed them, they had quickly recovered. He then shifted his gaze to the Queen's pavilion, where he espied William Cecil whispering something in the Queen's ear. It must have been something very amusing, since she first smiled and then laughed out loud.

In the meantime, the Master of the Joust had come over to Essex. "My lord of Essex, are you ready for your opponent?"

Essex took one last look at the Cecils—for Robert Cecil was seated behind his father, shielded as usual—and said, with the petulant, peevish tone of voice that knowledgeable people at court had learned to fear more than an out-and-out explosion of anger, "I'm ready—for all of them."

His page helped him onto his horse, and then handed him a new lance. While he rode to his place—and while his opponent did the same—the heralds brought their long trumpets to their lips and played their rousing jousting tune. The music died away and for a few short moments the field was as silent as the dawn of creation. Then the signal was given, and the pounding of the horses' hoof beats filled the place with a din of earthly thunder.

The two riders collided. This time Essex's opponent missed his mark, leaving an entry for the Earl to deliver a fatal blow. The opponent fell from his horse, and did not get up again. While the opponent's pages carried their fallen master off the field, Essex rode to the Queen's pavilion and saluted her. She nodded at him and smiled. Before he rode off, he gave the Cecils, father and son, a dark glance and noted with satisfaction that they were not as merry as they had been a few minutes before.

CHAPTER XI

William had not attended the jousting tournament. It was not that he disdained other forms of entertainment; he was simply too busy. It was hard work being the "new hope" of the London theatre, and he knew that he could not be "new" forever, unless he continued to surprise the audience with each new play and give them something that was truly novel. To remain the same was to fall backward, and to fall backward was to one day risk inhabiting the ale house seat of that malcontent Henry Chettle. Just the thought of it made William shudder.

Yet he felt as stale as a last year's loaf. He hadn't an idea in his head, not for a play and not for a sonnet. He had been staring at the same blank page all morning, and had nothing to show for it except a dull ache in his neck.

He went over to the window and opened it wide, hoping that a strong dose of bracing air would help. Below, the street was teeming, as usual, with life; it was a world rushing forward, and it all went so quickly, this thing called time. Already the street below him had changed, if not its scene then its cast of characters. New carters were coaxing their tired horses onward, new tinkers were shouting out their services. His thoughts wandered back to Stratford, where his son Hamnet was most likely sitting in the town's grammar school. Perhaps he was secretly carving his initials into the ancient wood of his desk at this very moment, just as William had done before him, not so very long ago.

He was still thinking about Stratford when there was a knock at his door. He half-expected his son to walk in, but the visitor wasn't Hamnet, although he was from Stratford.

"I'm on my way back home, Mr. Shakespeare," said one of the town's carters, whom William used as his messenger since the man was a trustworthy fellow. "Is there anything you wish to send to your family?"

William replied that he did have something to send. He wrapped several coins in a piece of cloth, along with a letter, and fastened the small bundle securely.

The carter, who was in his own way a sensitive person, hadn't looked while William counted out the coins. But he now appraised the bundle that rested in the palm of his hand with a judicious eye.

"I happened to hear your mother mention that your father has been served with another fine."

"For not attending church?"

The carter nodded. "Those fines add up at an alarming rate, seeing how there are so many Sundays in a year."

"Tell my mother that I hope to send more money next month."

"I'm sure she will be very glad to hear it. And if I'm not being too impertinent, sir, I think it would do your mother — and your children — a world of good to see you again. It's been a long time since we've seen you in Stratford."

"Yes, I hope to pay a visit soon." William took out another coin and gave it to the carter. "But I have a new play to write. It's hard to get away."

As the carter was leaving, another visitor entered.

"May I come in?" Richard Burbage asked.

"Of course." William brought another chair to the table, while Richard set down a load of books that he had been carrying. "What's all this?" William asked, picking up one of the volumes.

"Ideas for the new play. Father says he wants it to go into rehearsal next week."

"Next week? I haven't even started it yet."

"I thought as much, which is why I've come round to tickle your imagination and whip up your wit—and I'll spare you the other half-dozen hackneyed phrases that came from my father's mouth as he sent me on my way. But the play has got to be up and running before that Jew is executed."

"Don't you mean arrested?"

"That's bound to happen soon."

"And there has to be a trial."

"That's why you have to write the play now. We want to time the opening with the start of the trial. But the trial won't last long, from what I hear, and no one will be interested in our play after the Jew is executed, so let's get to work."

"How do you know the Jew won't be acquitted?"

Richard laughed. "Stop trying to procrastinate and start looking at these books."

William picked up one of the volumes and glanced at the title page. "*Decameron*—haven't we used this before?"

"Yes, and quite successfully. Apparently there's another story in it we might be able to use, something about a Jewish moneylender and a Moorish king."

"Wonderful. I know as much about Moors as I know about Jews."

"Nobody in the pit knows anything about them, either. So you're in good company."

Since Richard had settled himself comfortably in his seat, William did the same. "What's the plot?"

"According to our resident Italian scholar and translator, Angelo ..."

"And where would I would be without Angelo?"

"You'd be setting your love stories in England, and not Italy."

"I can't imagine anything duller than that."

Richard raised his eyes from the page of notes that he had been perusing and grinned. "You're obviously not spending your time in the right company."

"Never mind. What's the plot?"

"Why don't you come along with me tonight? One of my lady friends is giving a party."

"The plot?"

Richard tucked away his grin and went back to business. "In Angelo's opinion, there isn't much of a plot. It's just a discussion about three rings, and in the end the Moor and the Jew become friends."

"We can't have that." William tossed aside the book and picked up another. "*Il Pe – cor – ane*. What does that mean?"

"*The Simpleton*."

"That doesn't sound promising either."

"It's just the name of the book. But there is a story in it that might work. It's about a Jewish moneylender."

"Speaking of money, when is your father going to pay me what he owes me for the last two weeks' performances?"

"I thought he lent you some money a few weeks ago. Have you already spent it?"

"Yes."

"How?"

"The way most people do. I removed a coin from my purse and gave it to someone else."

"Who did you give it to? Most young men waste their money on drink or on their mistresses, but you don't do any of that. So where does your money go?"

"Never mind. Just tell me the story."

"Now that I think of it, I really don't know anything about you."

"Not true. You know that I have to write a play this week. The story?"

Richard magnanimously put aside his own curiosity for the sake of his father's theatre (he would remind his father of that fact at a later time, such as when his father was berating him for spending too much time with his lady friends and not enough time on the family business) and took another look at his notes, before saying, "It starts with a wealthy woman who lives in Belmont Castle and she has a husband who needs money – a man who needs money, that should speak to you, William. Hold on, you're not married are you? Secretly supporting a family of nine on your meager earnings from The Theatre?"

"Nobody wants to see a play about a married couple. What other books have you got there?"

"So you'll change it. Turn the husband into a lover." Richard's eyes lit up, tickled by his imagination. "That's it! He'll be a young lover who needs money to marry the wealthy woman he loves."

"Better," William reluctantly conceded.

"Now, a friend of the husband — I mean, the lover — goes to a Jewish moneylender ..."

"Moneylender, again?"

"What's wrong with that?" asked Richard.

"Nothing. It just seems that evil moneylenders are a recurring theme in these Italian stories, and I wonder why. Doesn't everyone chase after money? Wouldn't you rather be rich than poor?"

"Don't wander off the subject," said Richard, who knew very well that his father loaned out money to the company's actors and authors with interest, even though it was a crime to do so under English law. "The point is that if your Jew is a moneylender, he'll be different from Marlowe's Jew of Malta. So stop wasting time and listen to this. This Jewish moneylender agrees to lend the friend of the lover the money, but he demands a pound of flesh as payment, if for some reason the borrower can't pay back the loan."

"A pound of what?"

"Flesh."

William rolled his eyes.

"Well, why not?" Richard asked.

"Richard, what would you do if one day you woke up and discovered that you were a Jew?"

"Throw myself into the Thames."

"Be serious for a moment. Why is it that everyone is always so willing to believe the worst about the Jews? The author of this book, for instance, where did he hear this story? How do we know that it's not all a pack of lies? Have you ever heard of such a thing happening in real life? The theatre should hold up a mirror to nature. It should ..."

"Don't go off on a tangent again. A blood-thirsty Jewish moneylender will make for good drama. It will put warm bodies in The Theatre's cold and empty pit. Lots of bodies."

"You know how I hate it when writers hack people to pieces on the stage."

"You did it yourself in *Titus Andronicus*."

"Only because I was just getting my start. All this blood and violence — what does it have to do with art?"

"Not a thing, which is why you make more money from your plays than from your sonnets."

"When I get paid."

"You'll get the rest of your money when you hand in the new play."

"So that's it. Your father is holding my ducats ransom."

"William, I don't think you understand the seriousness of the situation. Every other theatre in London is already in rehearsal with their play about a Jew. If we don't have one, too, Father will be furious."

William stood up and struck a pose, to make a more powerful statement. "I'm sorry, Richard, but I cannot write a play about a pound of flesh. It's too gruesome."

"What do you do when you go to a public execution? Close your eyes?"

"I've never been to one."

"I'll take you with me to the Lopez show. They're saying he's going to get the full treatment — hanged, drawn, and quartered."

"In that case, a play about one miserly pound of flesh might be too tame for our audiences."

Richard scrutinized The Theatre's most promising playwright through his lazily half-opened eyes, which saw more than most people saw when their eyes were wide open. "What's gotten into you, William? You've never had so much trouble writing a play before. Why is this one causing you problems?"

"My heart just isn't in it."

"Banish it. Keep your thoughts focused on all those shiny ducats that will soon be filling your purse."

William sat down and reached for another book. "Isn't there anything else in this pile?"

"William, listen to me. No one cares if this one isn't a masterpiece. Just write something – anything – and Father will be happy. Besides, it will only be on the boards for a few months at most, and then it will be forgotten. Treat it as if you were asked to write a Christmas pageant for the Queen – a light entertainment, a merry jest."

"A jest?"

"Yes, why not?"

"Richard, what would you do if one day you discovered that I was a Jew?"

"I'd throw you into the Thames. Now, sit down and write. You've already got a good start: a rich heroine, a lover who needs money, and an evil Jewish moneylender who stands between them. All you have to do now is ..."

"I know. Fill the stage with dead bodies before the final speech."

ii.

Richard had gone, leaving William to fill up the blank pages. But there were more scratched out words than useable ones, and even he was beginning to wonder what was wrong with him. He couldn't even decide if the play should be a comedy or a tragedy. Every time he got going with a love scene filled with a suitable amount of fluffy poetry, the gruesome image of the pound of flesh intruded, casting a grisly, laugh-stopping pale over the proceedings. But when he tried to envision the play as a tragedy, he ended up laughing out loud. There just wasn't anything sublime about having a hunk of flesh hacked out of a person. A dagger to the heart, a sword run clear through the chest—those were noble ways to die. But carving up a person as if he were a side of beef was ludicrous. And so he went back to writing a comedy, for a while.

A modern psychologist might have offered the opinion that Mr. Shakespeare's problem was not just one of dramatic construction. In his subconscious mind, the image of the Catholic and the Jew had become blurred. Both were feared and despised in Protestant Elizabeth's England, which is perhaps why Richard Burbage could be so sure that the Portuguese-Jewish Dr. Lopez would be found guilty even before he was arrested and tried. The half of the doctor that was a Jew had a long history, at least in the public imagination, of being a poisoner of cups and wells. The half that had been a Portuguese Catholic, before the doctor turned Protestant, might have had a shorter history in the public mind as a master of rebellion, but it was a bloody one. Although not every Catholic in England was busy thinking up plots to kill the Queen, there were enough hotheads running about to heat up the epoch for everyone, including those who were only remotely connected to the old religion.

Or, perhaps it wasn't religion that was the problem, since William didn't consider himself to be a particularly religious man. He liked the old-time Catholic rituals and rites, which appealed to his sense of drama and mystery. But he also liked the more easy-going ways of the Protestants, who not only let the existing theatres remain open but encouraged the companies to produce their plays. So perhaps it was the topic of money that bothered him. Like the young lover of the play, William also needed money—not to marry, but to support his wife and children. He was also supporting his parents, now that his father had gone into a mysterious decline. John Shakespeare had grown almost childish during the last few years. Not only did he refuse to go to church, but he quarreled with his neighbors over nothing. And then there was the issue of the coat of arms. For some reason, the elder Shakespeare had gotten it into his head that he needed—nay, deserved—a coat of arms, and his son the famous playwright was going to help him get it. And it may as well be mentioned here—since if it is not, there are others who will whisper it about, anyway—that John Shakespeare had also been a moneylender, in Stratford, like the Jew in the story; what was more he had been prosecuted for the crime of lending money with interest. Perhaps, then, it was only natural that the son should feel squeamish about creating a villain whose despised profession so closely mirrored one practiced by his father.

A third possible interpretation, for those preferring to discard religion and money, was that it was the sting of the insult that prevented William from accessing his imaginative powers. Richard Burbage might have thought he was doing his playwright a favor by telling him that his play didn't have to be a masterpiece, but for an artist like William Shakespeare, that was the death knell. If it wasn't going to be a masterpiece, why bother to write it? He was no hack writer who aimed low to please the nether-most region of the pit. Any playwright, even Henry Chettle, could write a rabble-rousing play about a Jew. The world didn't need a William Shakespeare for that. No, for him to get excited about a new project, he first had to believe that he was about to do something great, something that would be remembered, preferably until the end of time.

It's very likely the psychologists and literary critics can think of other reasons why William could not progress with his story, but just because he is stuck in a creative quagmire there is no reason why our story must be stuck, too. Let us just say that a day passed, perhaps even two, and still he sat at his table, writing and scratching out, and writing and scratching out again. We will therefore leave him for a short while, and direct our gaze to, as the printers like to say, another part of the forest.

iii.

Robert Devereux, the 2nd Earl of Essex, might have had a fine and comfortable house on the Strand that was the scene of many a witty and sumptuous literary party, but there was no place that raised his spirits like London's infamous Tower. As he walked through the heartless stone corridors and past the prisoners' dismal cells, feeling very much the master of the place, he was like the modern-day child who has been given the keys to the biggest and best toy store in the world. Of course, he couldn't have known that just a few years later – on February 10, 1601, to be precise – he would be beheaded in that very same Tower. For how could he have known that he would be charged with treason by his arch enemy, Robert Cecil? (Ah, the sting of it, for it was old William Cecil's son who did become England's next Secretary of State.) Or, irony of ironies, that he would be accused of being sympathetic to the Catholic cause and tolerant of religious dissent?

He could not have known what fate had in store for him any more than any other man, and so he didn't bother his handsome head with thoughts about the future. Like most men of his time, he seized the opportunities that were set before him when they were within his reach and squeezed them for all they were worth before they disappeared. To worry that his life might be thrown away along with the pits and the peels was to be overcome with debilitating doubts – and no good could ever come of that.

He therefore entered the room where the rack held pride of place with a cheerful mien. Waiting for him was the prisoner, Senor Tinoco, and the prison warden who was an expert at operating the rack's system of chains and pulleys.

"Good afternoon, Senor Tinoco," he said, giving the prisoner one of his famous smiles. "I hope that today your memory will serve you better. Now, about those instructions concerning Dr. Lopez ..."

iv.

William's quill pen had grown dull, but instead of rushing to sharpen it with his knife he strolled over to the window. He had heard one of the street peddlers call out something about books, but in truth any excuse to take a break would have done. He saw that the calls were coming from a young boy, who was about Hamnet's age and loaded down by a heavy sack filled with ancient-looking tomes.

The child was calling out to the passersby, "Rare books! Unusual volumes from strange and various lands! Rare books!" But he was having no takers, despite his energetic cries. It was therefore perhaps only reasonable that when the boy spotted William at the window, looking down upon him, that he should direct his sales presentation to that quarter.

"Rare books, sir?"

"Not today. But here is something for your trouble."

William was about to throw the child a small coin. He didn't usually encourage the young street peddlers in this manner, but he was feeling in a generous mood, perhaps because he was grateful that his son Hamnet didn't have to work for his daily bread. But before the coin could leave his hand, the child called out, "I shall be right up!"

Since his generous mood didn't go so far as to invite the child to share his meal, William was standing in the hallway, blocking the entrance to his rooms, when the boy arrived at the top of the stairs.

"Mr. Shakespeare?"

"How do you know my name?"

"If you will let me inside, sir, I will show you a book that you will be proud to add to your library."

"I'm not interested. You've wasted your breath for nothing."

"I've got books in Latin, Greek and ... secret code."

"No, thank ... What did you say?"

The boy removed a book from his bag and opened it to a place that was marked with a handwritten note. William took the note and read: Henry Rivers, Bookseller.

"My father is waiting in his shop. It's not far."

"Your father?" William searched the boy's face for some sign of his childhood friend. He decided the boy must more resemble the mother, but there was something of Henry in the child's eyes, which were both bright with quick intelligence and gray as a stormy afternoon.

"Will you follow me, sir?"

William hesitated for a moment. He had not forgotten his childhood friend, but he hadn't thought about him either for quite some time. It was curious that at the moment when he had to write a play about a Jew that the only real Jew he knew should reappear in his life—was that a good or bad omen, he wondered? But he was also curious to see his friend after so many years and it was that curiosity which won the day. He therefore followed the boy through a warren of narrow, crowded, and twisting streets. However, the boy had spoken truthfully when he had said that the way was not far, and William wondered at the amazing circumstance that had placed both him and Henry Rivers in the same part of London, without either one of them being aware of the other's existence. Or, at least, William hadn't known about Henry. His friend, he supposed, by now must have heard of the playwright William Shakespeare, like everyone else in London.

The shop was no different than the other bookshops that William would often visit. Even though both James and Richard Burbage were always on the lookout for good stories to adapt for the stage, he also liked to thumb through the old histories and tales from other lands. He couldn't read foreign languages, but sometimes all it took was a vivid woodcut drawing to get his imagination going.

He recognized Henry at once. Even though a good dozen years had passed, and perhaps even more, he would know that sad, apologetic smile anywhere. Today it was because Henry was busy helping a customer choose a book and so he had to make his childhood friend wait. All those years ago it was because he couldn't join William at the River Avon to pretend they were going on a sea journey to discover the New World, or some other such game.

When the customer had made his purchase and left, Henry nodded toward a curtained doorway. "Let's go inside, William. It will be more private." He then turned to the child and said, "Simon, mind the shop."

Henry led William into a workroom. There were tools for binding books and fitting them with new covers. There was also a table set off to the side where a young woman was working with paints.

"This is Joan, my younger sister," said Henry. "I don't suppose you remember her. She came up to London a year after I did, after my father died."

Joan looked up from her work. "Good morning, Mr. Shakespeare," she said, while examining the visitor with unabashed interest.

"Surely it's William you mean to say. I yanked your hair too often for such formalities as Mr. Shakespeare."

Joan smiled, and then went back to her work. Her job was to color the illustrations that were sometimes found in books, and she could not leave her paints sitting too long if she wanted to have even colors.

"Does your wife also help you with your business?" asked William, looking around the room. He was naturally curious to see what sort of woman his friend had married.

"No, she's busy with the children. Are you married as well, William?"

William was about to reply, when his earlier uneasiness returned and stopped him. He had no reason to suspect Henry's summons for anything other than what it appeared to be on the surface—a wish for two old friends to renew their acquaintance—but London was such a strange place in those days. It seemed that every Earl and Lord was engaged in hunting out treasonous plots and employed a troop of spies and agents to achieve their aims. It was better not to reveal too much at first. He therefore changed the subject and said, "I suppose you don't get much news from Stratford."

"None at all, since Joan came to London and our stepmother remarried. I hope your father and mother are well."

William noted that Henry had followed his lead, as usual, and the topic of his marital state had been tactfully dropped. Yet he still wasn't sure if Henry was merely responding to his perceived reluctance to discuss the subject, or something else.

"My father's business concerns could be doing better," said William, "but both he and my mother are in good health."

"I am glad to hear it. And I am glad to hear that you are doing well, William. I don't go to plays myself, but I hear that yours are very good."

"Perhaps you will be willing to print some of them one day. Do you have a printing press?"

"Not yet. But we keep busy with the selling and binding and coloring."

William breathed in the heady aroma of glues and paints with pleasure. The closeness of the atmosphere might have bothered another, but he loved the world of books almost as much as he loved the theatre and to him the smells of the trade were as delightful as a perfume from Arabia—or so he supposed, never having actually come across such a scent.

"I like it here, Henry. I'm very happy that your profession is books and not ..."

There was an awkward silence. Even Joan's brush was suspended in mid-air.

Henry smiled his sad smile. "Moneylending?"

William could have rushed to reassure his friend that he hadn't meant that, but then they wouldn't really have been friends. And as he stood in the room and studied Henry's face, searching for and happily finding traces of the boy he had shared so many games and secrets with, a flood of memories—vivid scenes and even snatches of conversations—washed over William, reminding him that they had been friends, and friendship was a bond that must never be casually discarded.

"Yes, Henry, I am glad that you are a bookseller and not a moneylender. And I never told anyone about what happened that night. If I recall those days correctly, your father gave out the story that you had gone out to look for Old Isaac, without your father's knowledge, and that the two of you must have gotten lost in the storm. I never contradicted him. Even when people whispered that it was strange that there was no trace of either you or your grandfather, I didn't say a word. Joan can vouch for me."

He looked toward the young woman, who said, "I told Henry. I said that you could be trusted."

"Trusted?" William turned from the sister to the brother.

"I'm in trouble," said Henry. "If you don't wish to become involved, I'll understand. We'll shake hands and continue to go our separate ways. But if you do still have some feelings for an old friend ..." He let the sentence drift away, unfinished.

"I can't say I can help until I know what the trouble is. But I'm willing to listen."

"Thank you. It's best if we talk in this other room."

William watched as Henry walked to a cupboard and moved aside some books that were sitting on a shelf. Henry then removed a small piece of paneling, which revealed a lever hidden in the wall. When Henry pushed down on the lever, the cupboard swung to the side, revealing a passageway into another room. He motioned for William to follow him, and when they were both inside Henry closed the door, which seemed to disappear into the wall, so skillfully had the concealed entrance been constructed.

They were in a secret synagogue, although William didn't know it. All the Jewish ritual items were stowed away behind other locked doors, which were unlocked only when the small community of Conversos—Jews who had been forcibly converted to Catholicism in Spain and Portugal but had remained loyal Jews in their hearts—gathered in the room to pray. But even though William could not know for sure where he was, he suspected that the room was used for prayer; Catholics also had secret chapels hidden in their homes, as everyone knew.

"Henry, why are we meeting here like two conspirators?" asked William. "What exactly is this trouble that you're in?"

"You seem to remember that night when my grandfather died. Do you also recall that there was a doctor whom we met in the storm?"

"Of course, you went with him to London."

"Do you remember his name?"

William thought for a moment. "No, I'm afraid I don't."

"His name was Lopez, Dr. Rodrigo Lopez."

Although there were no glues or paints in this room, William felt his head begin to spin. He hadn't followed all the details of the assassination plot, but he knew enough to sense danger just at the mention of the physician's name.

"He's in trouble," Henry added.

"I know. It's all everybody is talking about."

"But he's been falsely accused. He'd never assassinate the Queen."

"How can you be so sure?"

"Dr. Lopez was in the employ of Francis Walsingham ..."

"The Queen's spy master?"

"Yes, Walsingham employed him as a double agent. His job was to pretend to be a spy for King Philip of Spain, but what he was really doing was passing on false information to the Spanish court."

"Henry, how do you know all this?"

"I helped him do it."

William stared at his friend. If it weren't all so deadly serious, he would have laughed. As children, he was the one who had played the starring role in their childish dramas about spies and secret plots. Now, here was Henry—quiet, retiring Henry—claiming that he was a spy in Her Majesty's Secret Service. For a moment, he thought that Henry would remove the serious mask from his face and laugh and say, "I've tricked you, William! I've got the better of you at last!" But his heart was telling him that this was no joke; his friend was in the kind of trouble that usually ended up in one place alone: the gallows.

"Why did you do it, Henry?"

"I was in the same position as Dr. Lopez. I had no choice."

"That's not true. Dr. Lopez is a foreigner. But you're an Englishman. You were born here. What hold could Walsingham possibly have had over you?"

"You forget, William. I'm a Jew. From the moment I joined the Converso community here in London, I was in Walsingham's power. It's been illegal for Jews to live in England since the year 1290. It's a crime punishable by death. The only reason why we're tolerated by the government and allowed to live here is because of our connection to Spain and Portugal, which Walsingham found useful."

"So why doesn't Dr. Lopez just say that he's really a double agent?"

"Because Walsingham has been dead for four years, and there's no one else who is willing to come forward and substantiate his claim. His only friend at court is the Queen."

"Surely that is worth something."

"For anyone else, it would be worth everything," said Henry. "But somehow it's always different when it comes to the Jews. And it doesn't matter a bit to Essex and the others at court that Dr. Lopez has converted again—this time to the Protestant faith—to win their favor. They still hate him, and this supposed Spanish plot to poison the Queen is just the opportunity they've been looking for to bring about his downfall. That's why I have to help him. I'm the only friend he has left."

William didn't know what to say. He sympathized with his friend's plight and admired Henry's loyalty to the physician. He remembered the doctor's kindness on that long-ago stormy night, and the good deed that Dr. Lopez had done when he buried Old Isaac. William supposed that he had also been kind to Henry when they arrived in London. If Henry was established in business and able to support his family comfortably and honorably, it was probably due to the assistance he had received from Dr. Lopez over the years. But all that was Henry's concern, and Henry's debt to repay. He didn't see where he came into the story, and he said as much to his friend.

Henry hesitated. Then he said, "I thought—that is, if you are willing to help us—I thought that you could write a play."

"What?"

"William, you have a gift for words. Your plays make the Queen laugh and they make her cry. Couldn't you use that gift to appeal to her sense of justice and mercy, so that she'll make Essex call off this ridiculous witch hunt and leave Dr. Lopez alone? Of course, you'd have to change the story."

William stared at Henry, wondering who was the crazier of the two. "Henry, I can understand why you feel obligated to help your friend, but you must listen to reason. Regicide is a capital offense. I can't—I won't—defend Dr. Lopez publicly, in the theatre. And you mustn't try to defend him, either. Think of your family—your wife, your sister, your son. What will happen to them if Essex finds out about your connection to the physician?"

"Believe me, I've thought of nothing else since this whole thing began. But if Essex has his way, Dr. Lopez is going to be executed. How will I explain to my son that I watched in silence as an innocent man was slaughtered—and one of my own people—and I didn't do a thing to try and stop it?"

"Before you asked me if I was married; now I'll answer you. I am married, and I have children, as well. They come first, Henry. I'm sorry."

William turned and was about to make his exit, when he recalled that the door could only be opened by the secret lever, which was once again hidden by its paneled covering.

"Don't worry, William, you're not my prisoner," Henry said as he walked over to the concealed lever. "But before we say goodbye, probably for forever, could I ask you one thing?"

William nodded his assent.

"I can understand that you feel no personal obligation to help Dr. Lopez. But as an Englishman and a man of letters, does not your conscience rebel at the thought of the State hanging an innocent man?"

"My conscience is clear precisely because I am an Englishman. We have laws in England, and courts of law and noble statesmen who are dedicated to upholding those laws. If Dr. Lopez is innocent the Privy Council will acquit him."

"Do you truly believe that?"

"With all my heart."

"Then perhaps you've forgotten that Essex is not only the head of his own branch of Her Majesty's Secret Service, but also a member of Her Majesty's Privy Council. That means he'll be one of the judges, and I can assure you that he is not going to dismiss his own evidence, flimsy as it may be. The only hope Dr. Lopez has is to obtain a pardon from the Queen. I know I'm asking you to take a risk – an extraordinary risk – but as long as no one suspects that you are personally involved, your play will look like it's an entirely innocent and spontaneous plea for mercy. The only crime that people will think to accuse you of is being the possessor of too kind and generous a heart."

William was listening with his ears, but his mind had drifted to somewhere else, to his own rooms, where earlier that day he had been discussing the Lopez affair with Richard Burbage. He recalled the way that Burbage, who came from impeccable Protestant stock, had so glibly assumed that Lopez would be executed. It was almost as if the doctor's innocence or guilt was an unimportant detail, insignificant as a piece of lint and less troublesome than a flea. It was true that a Jew was at the bottom of the rung in

England, but a Catholic accused of treason could not expect much from the State, either, in terms of mercy.

"You're forgetting something, Henry. My family is Catholic. A relative of my mother's, Edward Arden, was hanged for the very same crime, plotting to kill the Queen. If Essex sends his agents to Stratford, he'll find all that out in an hour. And once the Burbages find out about my Catholic connections, my career will be over."

"Yes, and it would be a pity if your career were cut short, since you've been given this tremendous gift. But do you truly believe that you are supposed to throw away this gift on frivolous entertainments—silly comedies and violent tragedies that serve no purpose other than to amuse a bored citizenry?"

"It's what the people want."

"But is it what you want? We're created for a purpose, William. If you truly believe that your purpose in life is a trivial one, I won't detain you any longer. But if you believe that you possess at least a spark of greatness, I beg you to at least consider that this opportunity—the chance to save an innocent man's life—might be precisely the reason why you were created."

CHAPTER XII

A n hour later, William and Henry were on their way to Holborn, where Dr. Lopez and his family lived in a fine house. It would be gratifying to be able to write that William rushed headlong into his destiny with great courage and high spirits, but there was a reason why Henry decided not to delay the meeting a moment longer than necessary. He did not trust William's steadfastness. Therefore, after their disguises had been procured — they were to be two laborers hired to repair some wainscoting in the Lopez mansion — they set off.

William felt ill at ease, vacillating between wondering if the disguise was too overdone or not done enough. But lest someone should wonder how it could be that a person who spent most of his waking life either performing on the stage or writing for it could feel so anxious about playing such a simple part, a simple reminder should suffice: in the theatre, the fallen actors rise and go out for supper after their performance is over; at the gallows, they do not.

Our playwright therefore worried and fretted all the way to Holborn, wondering why he had let himself be convinced to take part in what could only be a hopeless cause. Sometimes he silently argued that there was nothing really wrong with being a writer of Italian comedies, and a playwright could do worse than make a career of them. Even when he recalled that he had recently decided that he needed a new challenge, he was not cheered by this rapid response to his prayer. A writer did not have to murder to write about one, he reasoned; nor did he need to commit treason to portray a rebel in a convincing way. The challenge he needed was to further stretch the boundaries of the dramatic form, and not have his own poor, frail form stretched on the dreaded rack.

But to give credit where credit is due, despite his misgivings he did not turn back. Nor did he try to bolt into the crowd, and lose his companion in this way. He went forward. And even though it may perhaps be too much to say that because he did go forward, despite his fears and misgivings, he became the kind of man who could one day write a *Hamlet* or *Lear*, we can say that most probably he would not have reached those literary heights if he had taken the obscure, safe, and low road in life. More than our thoughts, it is the deeds we do that are stamped on our hearts and minds, turning our unformed personalities into the unique beings we eventually become.

When they arrived, the two "workers" were admitted into the Lopez mansion by a servant who seemed determined to see nothing. William, for his part, noticed practically everything. Although he got only a glimpse of the downstairs rooms as he and Henry were led through the grand entrance hall and down a long passageway to the library situated at the back of the house, he could see that the house's size and proportions befitted a personage who consorted with the Queen and her court. It had also been furnished by a person of taste, William noted, as he calculated the cost of a beautifully carved oak cupboard—for he had an interest in such things, since he sometimes dreamed of the day when he too would possess such a home. His eye was attuned, as well, to more practical considerations, noting that a large, ceiling-to-floor tapestry hanging in the hallway could make a decent hiding place, should the need arise.

That need became more impressed upon William's thoughts as they traveled deeper into the Lopez home. There was a scent of danger in the house, a feeling of something being a bit off—and William was certain that it wasn't just his imagination. He had the uneasy feeling that this was a place where everyone was ready to flee at a moment's notice, and he dearly hoped that Henry had arranged for their escape route as well.

The servant left them at the library door, after announcing their presence. Henry, who was on familiar terms with the master of the house, entered the room first, while William followed.

At first, William did not see Dr. Lopez. His memories of the physician, which were the memories of a boy, were vague, but he did recall a vigorous man with a steel grip and a commanding tone of voice; a man in his prime, a man who might have cut a valiant figure on the battlefield if he had chosen soldiering as his profession, instead of medicine. But that man was not in the room.

The man who was in the room was a gray-haired man at the threshold of old age who was richly dressed and whose face and body had the soft and rounded contours of a person accustomed to spending long hours at the dining table, with convivial company. That man smiled benignly at the two young men and said, "I have heard good things about your work, and so I hope you will not disappoint me. The section of the wall that needs repairing is small, but I expect the repairs to match the rest of the wall exactly. If you do not think you can do the work as I wish it to be done, please tell me now, before you begin."

During his speech Dr. Lopez and gone over to a side door, which led to a secondary hallway, and opened it. A servant nearly fell into the room.

"Ah, Bedgberry, it is fortunate you were passing by," Dr. Lopez said to the servant, still smiling benevolently. "I am expecting a shipment of aniseed, which has not yet arrived. Please go to the customs clerk's office and find out what has happened. Here is the address."

Bedgberry took the slip of paper and left, his face as blank as an unwritten piece of parchment. Dr. Lopez watched the servant retreat down the hallway for a few moments, and then he shut the door.

"I suppose you are wondering, Mr. Shakespeare, why I do not get rid of the man, if I know he is a spy. But it is my experience that there is no such thing as a servant who cannot be bought. Therefore, replacing him with someone else would accomplish nothing. And his replacement might turn out to be a better spy than Bedgberry, who thankfully isn't very successful." Dr. Lopez stopped, and then he asked, "It is Mr. William Shakespeare that I have the pleasure of meeting again?"

"Yes, although I wish we were meeting again under happier circumstances," William replied.

Dr. Lopez acknowledged his visitor's words with a small shrug. He then said, "I am sorry I cannot offer the two of you refreshments, but it would look odd, since you are supposed to be workers. But since you, Mr. Shakespeare, have mentioned the circumstances that are the cause of this second meeting, I can, instead, offer a few words of advice to you two young men, sound counsel that I have learned only in my old age, to my shame and my sorrow. We spend our lives courting the good opinion of others—flattering, cajoling, and offering empty words of praise—hoping to receive a few empty words of commendation in return. It is only in the end we discover that the only conversation that truly matters is the one that we have with our own conscience. I do not pretend to be a saint, Mr. Shakespeare. I have done my share of empty flattering to achieve my aims. But my conscience is clear concerning the accusations being brought against me. I would never murder our Queen. "

William had not intended to be rude, but he thought he had heard footsteps while Dr. Lopez was talking, and his head had jerked round in the direction of the door where Bedgberry had been discovered.

"Dr. Lopez, we cannot stay long and I believe that William is in more need of evidence than speeches," Henry said. "Shall we begin?"

Dr. Lopez glanced at Henry. It was just a small gesture, and William wasn't sure if the glance was one of irritation or hesitation, but William thought he noticed in it the hint of a hounded man who is growing weary of the chase.

"Did you tell him about the syrup, Henry?" asked Dr. Lopez.

"No, I thought I'd let you explain."

"Very well," said Dr. Lopez, who shrugged again and then returned to his benevolently smiling self. "As you know, Mr. Shakespeare, the Earl of Essex is under the impression that I have been hired by the King of Spain to assassinate our Queen. I believe you are also aware that Francis Walsingham, the Queen's spy master, hired me to work as a double agent. He entrusted me with that work because he knew that I would never betray our sovereign."

"Yes, I am aware of all this," said William.

"If my information is correct, Essex has not yet found solid proof to substantiate his suspicions. But he is an energetic young man and I am confident that the day will soon come when he will think he has finally found what he has been looking for: proof that I accepted a commission from the King of Spain to poison Queen Elizabeth. He will discover — thanks to his henchmen in the torture room at the Tower — that I told King Philip that I would do the deed by putting poison in Queen Elizabeth's syrup. If Essex weren't blinded by hatred and ambition, he would see this fantastic plot for what it really was — a ruse to thwart Philip's plans. But since everyone knows that Essex intends to use me as a steppingstone to further his political career, I must thwart his plans before he discovers the details of this old and ridiculous plot."

"I don't understand," said William. "How does syrup help to prove your innocence?"

"The Queen detests syrup. She won't touch the stuff. Everyone at court knows it. Saying I would put poison in her syrup was like saying I'd poison her chamber pot. My bargain with King Philip was totally worthless. It was just a joke."

"A joke?" William observed the man standing before him, and once again he felt a twang of dissonance, like a lute that has been inexpertly tuned. The doctor he remembered had been a serious man of few words. This man was a polished courtier who could speak as glibly about poisoning a monarch as repairing the wainscoting of a wall. William supposed that he should have been prepared for the change; he knew that Lopez was physician to the Queen and he knew that one couldn't be successful in that position unless the man was both a good doctor and a good companion, someone who could amuse the Queen with charming stories, as well as heal her ailments with charmed potions. Still, his instincts were once again telling him to be wary; he didn't want the joke to be on him. "I suppose the plot to assassinate Don Antonio, the Pretender to the Portuguese throne, was also a joke?"

"My job—the job that Walsingham forced upon me—was to devise imaginary plots to keep King Philip busy, so that he wouldn't hire someone else, someone who was willing to murder Don Antonio, and the Queen."

"You must make that clear." Henry, who had remained silent until then, now came forward. "The Queen must be made to laugh at these ridiculous accusations."

William could have commented that a playwright, no matter how talented, could never force anyone in the audience to do anything. Audiences were highly unpredictable. Sometimes they laughed at lines that weren't intended to be funny, while other times they sat like stones through brilliant bits of comedic business. But he was not there to give a lecture on the theatre. There was, however, a point that he did wish to clear up.

"Speaking of jests," he said, "if a Jewish moneylender were to make a contract to lend money to a person who wasn't Jewish, could he ask for a pound of flesh as payment should the borrower default on the loan?"

While Dr. Lopez stared at him, Henry asked, "Does this have something to do with the play about Dr. Lopez?"

"It might," said William. "So my question is, would this contract be valid under Jewish law if it had this stipulation, or should we assume that the Jew was making a joke and therefore the contract shouldn't be taken seriously?"

Henry looked to Dr. Lopez, who said, "I am a physician, not a rabbi. I don't know what Jewish law would say."

Henry also could not give a definitive answer. But he did comment, "In our prayers we do say, 'The soul is Yours, and the body is Yours.' It is God who gives a person life, and He is the only One who has the right to take that life away. Since God is the owner of a person's body, I assume it would be forbidden for a person to sell part of his body. It would be as if a person would say that if he can't pay back his loan, he'll give the moneylender his neighbor's house as payment. He has no right to make such a stipulation in a legal contract, since his neighbor's house isn't his to give. Does that help you, William?"

"Yes, I think it does."

"But getting back to our play," said Henry, "when the Jewish character pleads for mercy in the final scene ..."

"Final scene? What about the rest of the play?"

"You're the playwright, William. We leave it to you to fill in the rest. But the final scene must include the ring."

"What ring?"

Henry turned to Dr. Lopez and said, "You know the details better than I do."

Dr. Lopez removed a small pouch from its hiding place within one of his voluminous sleeves. From the pouch, he removed a ring, which he showed to William. "As proof of my loyalty, I tried to give our Queen this ring. She refused to accept it."

"However, if she saw a similar scene played on a London stage," Henry interjected, "and you had the stage queen accept a ring from her faithful Jewish servant's hand ..."

"Then perhaps our Queen Elizabeth would be moved to accept this ring from me, as well—and spare my life."

William looked from the two speakers to the ring itself. He was hardly the person to evaluate the worth of a gem, having little experience in such matters. He did see that the ring was graced with both a diamond and rubies, but he assumed that the Queen must have dozens like it in her jewel box. He therefore asked, "Does this ring have some special significance for the Queen?"

"Yes, it does," said Dr. Lopez. "It is the ring that King Philip of Spain gave me as a down payment ... to assassinate her."

"You accepted payment?" William began to back away, towards the door. It was a melodramatic gesture, to be sure, and he probably wouldn't have stooped so low as to have one of the characters in one of his plays do such a thing. But life is often not as perfect, or as heroic, as the theatre. He was scared—and he couldn't have been more frightened if the physician had casually mentioned that there was an outbreak of plague in his house. "Henry, why didn't you tell me?"

"I assumed you knew how these political intrigues work. You are the author of *Richard III*, aren't you?"

"If I were you, Dr. Lopez," said William, ignoring the jibe, "I would forget about this play. You must try to win the assistance of William Cecil. Surely Essex can't do anything to harm you without his consent."

"Do you think I have not tried? Do you think I have not appealed to him to petition the Queen to stop this investigation?"

"They refuse to help," said Henry. "William Cecil's only concern is that his son Robert will become Secretary of State, and Robert is only concerned about himself."

"Mr. Shakespeare, I had to accept this ring. If I had refused payment, King Philip's suspicions would have been aroused and the whole stratagem would have failed. It signifies nothing."

"I still think it would have been better to displease the King of Spain than the Earl of Essex."

"I am a physician, not a prophet. I could not know that Walsingham would die so suddenly, or that this old plot—for it is an old plot—would re-emerge after so many years."

"If Essex ever finds out about that ring, you'll hang."

"Unless the Queen pardons him," said Henry. "William, you must believe us. You must believe me. I would never have asked you to become involved if I wasn't absolutely certain that what Dr. Lopez has said is the truth."

"I wish I could be as certain, Henry, but I can't. Good day, Dr. Lopez. I wish you success."

William turned to go, but before he reached the door Dr. Lopez called after him. "Mr. Shakespeare, just a word more, if I may."

"Only a word, Dr. Lopez, I really must get back to The Theatre. I'm already late, for rehearsal."

"I will try to be brief. Mr. Shakespeare, I've done everything to be accepted by this country. I've abandoned my God and my people. I've handed over my children to their churches and their schools. And I've served this country faithfully, both as the Queen's physician and a spy for her Secret Service. For all this, I've asked for only one thing in return—that I and my family be allowed to live in peace. The Queen must take notice of my plight. She must have mercy. She can banish me from England today, if that will appease Essex. But I'm an old man. How long will I be able to stand up to his tortures if he puts me on the rack? God, I didn't sell my soul for this!"

William watched uncomfortably as the physician collapsed onto a chair and began to sob. "You don't understand," he said, to both Henry and the doctor. "It's not so simple to write a play. I don't work alone. I'm only a shareholder in the company, not the owner. The others would have to agree, and there's the Censor—he'd have to approve the play, as well."

"We're not worried, William," said Henry. "If it's your play, it's sure to win the approval of them all—and win the heart of the Queen."

"Yes, but ..."

This time the sound of approaching footsteps was not William's imagination. Both Henry and Dr. Lopez looked to the main door to the library, as well.

Dr. Lopez, who had regained control of his emotions, sprang up from his chair and walked quickly to the wall behind his desk. At his touch, a piece of the paneling opened and he gestured to Henry and William to make a hasty retreat.

Henry, who was always prepared for such an event, was already at the opening. William followed. "What about you, Dr. Lopez?" he asked as the physician replaced the piece of wainscoting.

"It's too late," he whispered, and then the passageway grew dark.

While Henry silently led William through the dark labyrinth that eventually wended its way to an exit to the street, the door to the library was flung open and an exultant Earl of Essex, accompanied by a retinue of his Secret Service agents, entered the room.

"You're under arrest, Dr. Lopez." The Earl then said to his men, "Search the house. Tear it to pieces if you must. Whoever finds those 50,000 crowns first will receive a knighthood for his pains."

ii.

Since they dared not attempt to light a flare, it took Henry and William some time to reach the door that led to the street and their freedom. Dressed as they were in their laborers' garb, Henry felt confident that they could disappear into the crowd that was milling about the always busy thoroughfare. William was more inclined to try leaping onto rooftops and thereby avoid the agents that were surely at their posts outside of Dr. Lopez's house. But since he wasn't athletically inclined — that was Kempe's area of expertise — he followed his friend round to the front of the house, trying to mimic Henry's casual gait.

They reached the street at the same time that the front door to Dr. Lopez's home opened. Dr. Lopez, who was being held by two agents, was shoved into a waiting wagon. The Earl of Essex, who was giving some final instructions to one of his agents, followed a little behind. A crowd had already gathered in the street by the time Essex mounted his horse, but even so, Henry and William remained in a recessed doorway on the other side, where they could see but hoped they would be out of the Earl's sight.

Essex commanded the wagon driver to proceed, as gaily as if he and his party were about to embark upon a pleasure cruise on the Thames.

And then they were gone.

CHAPTER XIII

William made it back to his rooms without incident. He quickly changed into his own clothes and thrust the disguise he had been wearing into the back of a cupboard. He would return the clothing to Henry later, or perhaps Henry's son would come round for them. He glanced down at the manuscript pages that littered his table, at the pen and ink that sat upon that same table; everything was the same as he had left it. But he knew that he would get no more writing done that day. His thoughts were too jumbled and his nerves were too frazzled for such work, which required calmness and clarity of vision.

But to sit in his room and do nothing but stare at the four walls—and wait for the sound of footsteps, whether real or imaginary—was also impossible. He therefore set out for The Theatre, where he might be in time to see the end of that afternoon's performance of *The Two Gentlemen of Verona*.

James Burbage was seated in the counting room when he arrived. Peals of laughter could be heard coming from the stalls, which lay behind the closed doors.

"Another full house, William," James Burbage called out happily. "You're a genius, that's what you are, a genius with the golden touch."

"Thanks very much," William replied, trying to sound as natural as possible. He knew he was probably being ridiculous for thinking that one of Essex's agents might have recognized him on the street in Holborn and was following his steps, but there was nothing wrong with being careful and trying to appear that the Lopez affair was the furthest thing from his mind. "Then you won't mind paying me the money you owe."

"Maybe tomorrow, I haven't finished with the accountings yet."

"Then what about half?"

"Can't you see that I'm busy, William? This isn't the time."

"Then what about a loan?"

"The usual ten percent?"

William nodded. Nothing could be ordinary than for him to ask his employer for a loan. "The usual."

While James Burbage was counting out the money, a stagehand rushed into the room. Since the man, whose position was a lowly one, usually wasn't allowed admittance to the counting room, his initial haste was checked by the shiny columns of coins sitting on the table, a sight that filled him with reverent awe.

"Well, what is it?" Burbage scowled.

"It's Mr. Kempe, sir," replied the stagehand, recalling his purpose. "His costume has caught on fire."

"What? What? What?" Burbage shouted, jumping up from his seat even as terror gripped his soul. Already in his imagination he could see his precious, timbered theatre enveloped in flames.

"I'll take care of it," said William, and he left with the stagehand.

"Fire? Fire?" Burbage sputtered as he collapsed back into his chair. With a shaking hand he poured himself a cup of ale, which he swallowed in one gulp. "Not my theatre. Please, God, don't burn down my theatre."

Meanwhile, William had followed the stagehand around to the back of the playing area, from where he could see the stage. The bottom of Kempe's costume was on fire and the clown was running around the stage in a panic. The dog that was "playing" the role of Crab was running after Kempe, barking his head off with excitement. Another stagehand, carrying a bucket of water, which was splashing all over the stage, was running after Kempe and the dog, trying to catch up with them.

The audience roared.

ii.

"I've never been so frightened in my life." It was after the performance. Kempe and Richard Burbage and William were sitting in their usual places in the ale house. The dog Crab had joined them, against the protestations of Kempe, who was saying, "I give you my oath, William, I love you like a brother, but I'll never, never share the stage with that dog again."

Crab opened his mouth to protest, but Richard spoke for him. "Kempe, put it behind you and make up with Crab."

"That's easy for you to say, Mr. Burbage. It wasn't your behind that was nearly charred to a piece of burnt meat."

"I still don't understand how it happened," said William.

"It was like this," said Kempe, warming to his subject. "There I was, in Verona, making my entrance as I always do, the very Launce of a man, with the dog's leash in one hand and the lantern in the other ..."

"Why did you add a lantern? That's not in the text."

"So you're taking the part of the dog, are you? Then perhaps you'll play the role of Crab at tomorrow's performance, instead of that cur."

Crab growled his displeasure.

"I just asked a simple question," said William, ready to growl himself. If there was anything he hated more than actors who "improved" his dialogue it was clowns who destroyed the balance of a scene by adding too much low comedy.

Richard, playing his usual role as mediator, said, "He added some business using the lantern."

"I'll say he did. He nearly burned down The Theatre."

"Whose tale are you two interested in?" Kempe interrupted. Pointing to the dog, he said, "His, or mine?"

~ 151 ~

"Yours, Kempe, yours," said Richard.

"So there I was on stage, when I turned to my fellow player ..."

"The dog?" asked William.

"Nay, my good man. I too thought Crab was a member of a dogged race. But I discovered to my peril that under his furry, flea-bitten skin lays the coldblooded heart of a jealous, scheming, treacherous thespian."

Crab was about to protest this insult to his character, when William asked, "So, what happened next?"

"I said my line, without malice, and exactly as it was written in the text. Not a word more or less."

"That's a rare wonder. I'm sorry I missed it."

"And then," Kempe continued, "just as I was enjoying my well-earned round of applause, this jealous dog of an actor becomes bitten by a spirit of frenzy, jumps at my person, grabs me by the seat of my doublet, and sends me hurtling downward to the nethermost world, where a fearsome furnace was blazing like a towering torch."

"In short," said Richard, "the dog bit him and Kempe fell down and landed right on the lantern."

In spite of himself, William laughed.

"You find it amusing, do you, Mr. Shakespeare?"

"Yes, Kempe, I do."

"Then you're as heartless as he is." Kempe pointed his finger at the dog.

"Come, Kempe, enough," said Richard. "Make peace with Crab. See he begs for mercy."

Richard held together Crab's two front paws and Crab, who truly was more ham than dog, did his bit by howling piteously.

"Very well," said Kempe, shaking Crab by the paw. "It's lucky for you, Mr. Crab, that I'm in a magnanimous mood."

Richard let the dog jump down to the floor, to enjoy its meal of scraps, and turned his attention to William. "Now that Verona has been saved from strife, what's the news on the Rialto?"

"What?"

"The play, William, the one you're supposed to be writing."

"Make sure it has a good plot, something with plenty of action," said Kempe.

"And a good villain," Richard added.

Kempe nodded his head. "I miss Marlowe. Poisoned nuns, butchered lovers, and that Jew Barabas getting dunked into a bubbling cauldron of scalding water — that's entertainment!"

"It's too bad for The Theatre that I'm not Christopher Marlowe."

"Don't worry, William, I'll help you think of ideas," said Kempe. "But it's going to be hard to top throwing a Jew into boiling water. That was a real crowd pleaser."

"That might depend upon the crowd a person associates with."

"*The Jew of Malta* was one of the biggest money-makers of the 1589 season," said Richard.

"Marlowe knew how to throw the dogs a bone," Kempe agreed. "It's a pity he died so young." Kempe took a moment to assume a sad face and sigh. He then turned to William and said, "And remember, William, not so many words. When you kill off someone, there's no need for a long speech. Just let him die and move on to the next corpse."

William was about to suggest that perhaps Kempe might feel more comfortable joining the dog Crab under the table, when James Burbage rushed into the ale house, gesturing wildly.

"Quiet! Everyone! Quiet!" he yelled out.

A few of the patrons helped the elder Burbage up onto a table, so that he could better command the attention of the room. "Friends, theatre patrons, countrymen, set down your tankards and listen. Lopez the Jew has confessed! He's confessed to plotting to assassinate the Queen!"

The short silence that had descended upon the ale house was dispelled in a moment as everyone excitedly discussed the news. James Burbage jumped up and down on the table to get back their attention. "Let's drink a toast to our good, brave, English Earl of Essex. Publican, this round is on me!"

The crowd cheered a second time and the ale house owner made haste to fill all the glasses.

"To the Earl of Essex!" Kempe called out, raising his glass.

"To the Queen!" James Burbage yelled back at him, raising the glass that had been placed in his hand. "May she live and reign for many long and prosperous years to come!"

The tavern's patrons echoed the toasts and sounds of "To Essex! To the Queen!" could be heard throughout the room.

Richard, who had been watching William's face lose its color, poured some ale into the playwright's cup and said, "To the Queen, William."

William raised the cup. "To the Queen."

iii.

Richard Burbage had decided that he must keep a close watch on his playwright. Now that Dr. Lopez had confessed, time was of the essence. But the next morning, when he turned up at William's door, he was surprised to hear from the landlord that William had left his rooms at dawn. Since the landlord could provide no information about where William had rushed off to at such an ungodly hour—the last time that Richard had arisen at such an hour was when he was still a suckling child—Richard had no choice except to utter a mild oath and leave.

Meanwhile, William was on his way to Stratford. He had hired a horse, despite the expense and the fact that he was not an expert at the equestrian art. He was also traveling without a permit, which posed a more serious danger than falling off his horse. But he, too, knew that he had no time to lose. He would have to make a decision, and he only hoped that this trip home would help him make it.

When he arrived in Stratford several days later, he was exhausted, famished, and covered with dust. Indeed, his bedraggled appearance gave his mother a fright. But after he assured her that he wasn't a fugitive from the law — at least, not yet, he silently mumbled — she calmed down enough to sit him by the fire and order the servant to prepare a hot meal and put fresh linens on the first-best bed in the guestroom, a room that William sometimes used after an argument with his wife. William was in no state to demur, and he accepted the hint to expect a domestic quarrel in silence.

"Is Anne not here?" he asked.

"She took the children to visit her parents."

"And father?"

When his mother didn't reply, he asked, "At the alehouse?"

"You'll hardly recognize him, William. He sits there all day, and from what I hear all he talks about is that coat of arms. Can't you do something? It would make him so happy. And it would be good for the children."

"How are they?"

Mary Arden Shakespeare, who had had no one to unburden herself to for some time, unburdened herself now. "It's hard for them, William, especially for Hamnet. If your father was still an alderman, a respected person in town, it might be different. But with your father being what he is, and you away in London all the time — well, you know what children are, how they tease and fight and hurt one another. Anne and I can take care of the girls, but there's no one to stand up for Hamnet and I'm afraid he feels it. He's a sensitive child, too sensitive for his own good."

"Do you really think a coat of arms would help him?"

"I think he needs a father, William. But he isn't going to have one, is he? So a coat of arms will have to do, instead. At least it's something. I ... I think I smell something burning in the kitchen. Please excuse me, William."

Nothing was burning in the kitchen. William had a nose, too. He had eyes, as well, and they too were welling up with tears, stung by the knowledge of the sorry state his family had descended to.

After he had eaten and rested, he went for a walk in the town. When he reached the ale house, he glanced inside and saw his father, who seemed to wear his life's disappointments on his face like a wrinkled and soiled garment, sitting and chattering happily with a small crowd of ne'er-do-wells whose pockets were empty but whose hearts were also full of complaints.

Although William had been prepared to see his father changed, he was still troubled by the sight. It was not a portrait that he wished to resemble when his own life was approaching its final years.

He turned away. Wandering aimlessly, his steps took him out of the town and into the countryside. He barely noticed what crops were growing or which animals were grazing in the fields, because observing the external world was not his purpose. Instead, he wanted to think, to delve into his innermost being and discover the truth about who he really was. But everything seemed to oppress him; even the airy canopy above, which was miles away, seemed to press down upon him like a heavy weight. That was in contradistinction to what he had hoped to find in Stratford, the scene of his youthful hopes and dreams, the setting for the time when the sky was the only limit to what he had hoped to achieve—and he had wanted to have it all, then, fame and fortune and everything else that life had to offer.

Now, he wasn't so sure. He had seen another side of fame, and he didn't think he liked it; the side where people took notice of a person not to sing his praises but to see how they could use him to further their own aims. Sometimes the person was raised up, sometimes he was cast down, and there didn't seem to be any way to stop the wheel from turning, once it was set in motion.

Perhaps it might have helped if he had been willing to put into words the nebulous thought that was burdening his mind. But no man likes to admit that he is a coward, that he is brave on the shadowy battlefields of the imagination, but lacks conviction when life confronts him with a real and dangerous adversary. It's always much easier to rail against the slings and arrows of outrageous fortune than to say, "This is the hand that I've been dealt. Something is required of me. What is the noble thing to do?"

For those who might be wondering, suicide was not in his mind. He was, at heart, a man of the countryside, and not to the palace born. It was not melancholy, a feeling that working folk might have but can seldom indulge, which was preventing him from making his decision, which was this: should he write the play that would please his childhood friend and possibly help defend the physician and perhaps earn him a place in the annals that recorded the names of those few courageous souls who rebelled against bigotry, brutality, and oppression at the expense of their own lives; or should he write the play that his theatre company expected, and which might play a hand in sending the physician to his death, but would save his own neck?

No, there was nothing luxuriously languid about what he was feeling at that moment. Instead, every fiber in his body was sizzling with a burning anxiety that was giving him no rest, spurring him on to do something, take action, decide yes or decide no, stop the vacillating and make a decision.

He had reached the cottage, the place where he had spent so many happy afternoons listening to Old Isaac's stories. He peered through the little window—he could reach it now without having to stand on the tips of his toes—and looked inside. Apparently no one else had moved in, since it looked the same as the night when they had all left it.

William went inside and walked about the room, inhaling the not entirely unpleasant fragrance of old wood and dried thatch. The hearth was dark and cold, of course, but the table and stools were still there. He sat on one of the stools and closed his eyes.

Henry, did I ever tell you about the time I was captured by pirates? He could hear Old Isaac's voice as though he had gained admission to that story-filled room only yesterday.

Pirates?! His own childish voice exclaimed.

It's a pity, William, you don't want to hear that story. It's a good one.

But I do!

He's a spy. Father must have sent him. That was Henry's voice, and the memory of his friend's accusation still stung.

No he didn't. Nobody sent me.

Then what are you doing here?

I didn't tell about the secret code! I promise!

Don't worry, William, Old Isaac was saying. *I believe you. But a grave injustice has been done. So what shall we do?*

We must go inside ...

"And correct it," William whispered.

CHAPTER XIV

When William returned to London it was by carriage — another expense — and he instructed the driver to take him straight to The Theatre. After they arrived and he paid the driver the remainder of his fare, he turned and got a shock. A new announcement had been plastered onto the theatre's wall, which read:

OPENING NEXT WEEK!

A NEW COMEDY
BY
WILLIAM SHAKESPEARE

STARRING
RICHARD BURBAGE
AS

THE JEW

While William was still staring at the placard, he felt a man's hand grab him by the neck and roughly turn him around.

"Where in the devil have you been?" Richard Burbage hissed.

"And what the devil is that?" William pointed to the placard.

"I had to tell my father something to explain your absence, so I told him I locked you in your room so that you'd finish the play. William, I can't believe you did this to us. Don't you know that hell hath no fury like a theatre manager without a hit play? I don't know what my father is going to do when he sees you. "

"Thank me, I hope," William replied, handing Richard a thick manuscript wrapped in cloth.

"What ... It's not ...?"

"It is."

"What's it called?" Richard excitedly tore off the protective covering. "*Jest in Venice*. It's not bad. Venice, at least, will draw in the people."

"Are the others inside?"

"No, there was nothing to rehearse. But I'll have the speeches copied at once. We can get started rehearsing one or two scenes today."

"Richard, I think you should know ... about the play ..."

"Tell me later, William. I want to let Father know the good news."

ii.

The job of copying out a play's speeches for the actors required some skill, but not much. The person entrusted with the task needed to know how to recognize the letters and replicate them, but it was not part of his duties to understand what he was copying and comment upon it, or make corrections. Indeed, if the person were to take the time to actually read the text, it would only slow him down.

William therefore left the copier at his task while he completed one of his own. He hadn't bothered to disguise himself before he entered Henry's bookselling establishment. There was no reason why a playwright shouldn't wander into such a place, he had decided. But he understood why Henry turned pale. Fortunately, there were no other customers in the shop to see it.

A few moments later, William was once again in the back room. It looked the same, although Joan's face was expressing astonishment at seeing him, as well.

"I've written the play," he told them, keeping his voice low. "Is there any news?"

"William, don't be a fool. It's too late," said Henry.

"I asked if there is any news."

"The trial will be soon. You know that he confessed to promising to poison the Queen for 50,000 crowns?"

"Yes, I heard."

"He tried to convince Essex that he didn't mean to really do it. That he made the promise with Walsingham's knowledge and permission."

"And I'm sure that Essex believed him."

"Of course, he didn't."

"We can be ready by next week with the play. I just have to convince the company to stage it. After I've done that, and we have the public on our side ..."

"William, it's too dangerous. It would be one thing if the Cecils were with us. At least then it would be a fair fight. But the trial is just a formality, now that Essex has the confession."

"Someone has to stop that man. Someone has to stop all of them. Someone has to stop this culture of hatred and violence and lies, before it destroys us all, everyone single one of us."

"It's too late."

"The Queen can still pardon him."

Henry noticed that there seemed to be a manuscript hidden within the folds of William's cloak. "Is that the play, William? Let me have it."

William handed over the bulky package. Without bothering to unwrap it, Henry tossed the whole thing into the fire.

"But, Henry ..." Joan rose from her seat and went over to her brother.

"I won't let him do it," Henry said to his younger sister.

William smiled. "I knew you would try to stop me, Henry, but all you've done is burn to ashes a perfectly good sheaf of blank manuscript pages. The play is already at The Theatre, being copied. Rehearsals begin this afternoon."

He turned to go, but his path was blocked by Joan, who had rushed to reach the doorway before him. "Mr. Shakespeare ... William," she said to him, "thank you."

iii.

The rehearsal was in progress. Rehearsals are generally not a happy time. Perhaps the actors and the stage managers like to pretend that everything is going well and that they enjoy forgetting their lines and bumping into fellow actors who are standing in the wrong place, but pretending is their job. That's not to say that there aren't moments of joyous inspiration. But for every such moment there are dozens more that are tortuous in their execution, as the play is cut and wrenched into passable shape before the first performance begins.

William therefore tried to pretend that the air of hostility in the theatre was no different from the atmosphere of rehearsals for previous plays, when all had come right at the end. But he couldn't help but notice that even the dog Crab seemed to regard him with a disdainful eye, as though to say, "I'm glad there's no part for me in this one!"

He was still waiting for the proper moment to explain the play and what he hoped to accomplish with it. But the first day of rehearsals was always filled with a myriad of questions and tasks. And Richard and his father had been in a hurry to start blocking the scenes that had been copied.

Therefore, that was what they were doing now, with William playing traffic manager, as he said, "Richard, you and Bassanio should be standing downstage. And Richard, try saying your line while Antonio makes his entrance."

"All right," said Richard, who was playing Shylock. "Everyone ready?"

The two other actors nodded their heads, and Richard read from his page. *"Rest you fair, good signior! Your worship was the last man in our mouths!"*

"Shylock, albeit I neither lend nor borrow by taking nor by giving excess, yet, to supply the ripe wants of my friend, I'll break a custom." The actor playing Antonio turned to the one playing Bassanio and continued, *"Is he yet possessed how much ye would?"*

"Ay, ay, three thousand ducats," said Richard as Shylock.

"And for three months."

"I had forgot – three months ..."

"William! Not so many words!" a voice called out from the pit.

"What?"

Kempe came onto the stage. "We know the loan is for three months."

"He's right, William," said Richard. "You've already mentioned it in this scene six times."

"Shylock forgot."

"Well, that's too bad," said Kempe, "because the pit knows, and the gallery knows, and even the dog Crab knows that the loan is for three months. And they're all going to be asleep, drunk, or dead before I've said my first joke."

"Who's writing this play, me or you?"

Richard stepped between them and said, "Admit it, William. The scene is too slow."

"That's because we haven't gotten to the pound of flesh yet. That's when the scene picks up. It'll be very funny."

"It'll be so funny, we'll all be laughed out of town," said Kempe. "A pound of flesh. Really, William, I give you my oath, this is the dumbest play you've written yet."

"It's supposed to sound ridiculous, to show that Shylock wasn't serious when he made the agreement. It's a joke."

"A joke?" asked Richard.

"I don't hear anyone laughing," said Kempe.

Richard, who was usually unperturbed by a rocky first rehearsal, began to look seriously worried. "William, it can't be a joke. If the Jew isn't serious about demanding his pound of flesh, there's no play."

"You haven't read the entire play yet. Can we please continue with this scene?"

"If you're telling me the devil's bargain was a joke, there's no point," said Richard. "You have to rewrite it."

"I know I'm taking a bit of an artistic risk, but ..."

"It doesn't work."

"I'm not changing it, Richard. I'm the author and ..."

At this point James Burbage, who had just finished reading through the entire play, joined the group on the stage, carrying the manuscript in his hand. "You're the what?"

"Father, let me handle this," said Richard.

"This play has more problems than Crab has fleas." James Burbage began to thumb through the pages of the play. "Take a look at this speech, Richard."

"Which speech, Father?"

"This one." James Burbage showed his son the page. "This hath not a Jew eyes business. I can't make heads or tails of it."

Richard quickly looked through the speech, frowning while he read.

"Let me see it," said Kempe. Richard handed him the page, and Kempe began to read the speech aloud. "*Hath not a Jew eyes? Hath not a Jew hands, organs, senses, affections, passions? fed with the same food, hurt with the same ...*" It's too many words, William."

William grabbed the page out of Kempe's hands.

"Don't misunderstand us," said Richard. "I've read a few of the other scenes, and some of the writing—especially in the scenes with the two lovers—is very good. But this Shylock character that you've created ... I don't understand what you're trying to accomplish with this play."

"You'll understand when you've read the whole thing."

"I want to understand now."

"I'm trying to make a point."

"What point?"

"That the Jew is human."

James Burbage's mouth dropped open. "Human?" he blurted out. "Who wants to see a play about a Jew that's human?"

"All London will if we do it right."

"I've treated you like a son," said James Burbage, still in shock, "and this is how you repay me? Hath a Jew not eyes, indeed! I'll tell you who's got eyes. I've got eyes and do you know what I see? I see that every theatre in London is going to be making money from the Lopez scandal, except us. Even Christopher Marlowe has a play about a Jew opening this week, and he's been dead for a year. "

"You said you wanted me to write a play about a Jew, Mr. Burbage, and you've got one."

"I said? The play I commissioned from you was supposed to be about a wicked, cruel, evil, despicable, churlish and contemptible Jew! Not a Jew who's human and goes and gets himself pardoned!"

"What?" Kempe and Richard said in unison, like a Greek chorus.

James Burbage showed the two actors the final scene of the play. When they were done reading, Kempe looked up and said, "William, have you gone mad?"

William, realizing that his moment had come, steeled his courage and strode to the center of the stage, where he had a view of the entire company. "Mr. Burbage ... Richard ... Don't you all see? We have an amazing opportunity to do something entirely new. While every other theatre in town is busy concocting ridiculous plots about impossibly wicked Jews and manipulating the truth until there's nothing left but a heap of worn and ragged lies, we'll show our audiences something they've never seen before: a portrait of a Jew who is a living, breathing human being. We'll cast away the old stereotypes and tired prejudices and show them the grandeur — the nobility — of a people that has remained true to their traditions despite hardship and oppression. Of course, Shylock has his faults, and in the play he makes a tragic mistake—that's where the drama comes in. But is there anyone among us that has never stumbled and fallen? And having fallen is there a person alive who does not tremble at the thought of judgment and hope for mercy with all his heart? For God's sake, let us appeal to the good that is in each one of us, and in every Englishman. Let's extinguish, on our stage, the fires of envy and hate that demean the hater as much as they destroy the one who is hated. Let's demand justice and mercy for the Jew, and not his blood. If we do this, I promise you ... our play will be talked about in every mansion and ale house in London ... Everyone will want to see it. ... Well? ... Doesn't anyone have anything to say? ... Richard?"

William looked at Richard Burbage with pleading eyes, but the look he received in return was not an encouraging one.

"Rewrite the play."

William stood his ground, literally, and remained glued to his spot in the center of the stage. "Dr. Lopez is innocent. I have proof."

"I don't care." Richard, who kept his voice calm, slowly moved forward, like a gamekeeper moving in to trap a wild animal that has escaped from its cage.

"You must care," William protested. "We're Englishmen. We're men of culture and letters. If we don't demand justice, who will? Someone has to take a stand."

"But not us." Richard, who had reached the stage's center by this time, slowly placed his two hands on William's shoulders and looked William in the eye. "Rewrite the play."

"I'm not changing it."

There was a tense silence and then Kempe said, "Well! This beats everything."

"Kempe, stay out of this," said Richard.

"I won't be quiet," said Kempe. "I'm also a shareholder in this company. I can make speeches, too."

Kempe grabbed a woman's wig from one of the actors and put it on his head. From another actor he snatched a fake dagger, and from a third he took a red scarf, which he stashed into Richard's doublet.

"What are you doing?" asked Richard.

"Get over here, Richard," said Kempe, taking a position downstage. "Mr. William Shakespeare isn't the only dim-witted playwright in London. If this theatre absolutely must put on a foolish play about a Jew and a pound of flesh, I say let's have a competition. Let the company decide whose play they prefer—yours, Mr. Shakespeare, or mine."

While the rest of the company took their places to watch the performance, Kempe jumped onto a chair and said, "Gentlemen, and not so gentle men, I give you the Tragedy of Antonio and Shylocket, the Stupidest Pair of Lovers That Ever Lived." He then motioned for Richard to take his position below him, and said, with a simpering voice, "Antonio, Antonio, wherefore art thou, Antonio? Deny thy father and refuse thy name. And for that name, which is no part of thee, take all myself."

"I take thee at thy word," Richard declaimed, since the part of Romeo was still fresh in his mind and he thought a good laugh would defuse the tense situation. "And for that word, give all my heart."

"All your heart?" asked Kempe, batting his eyelashes with amazing speed.

"It's yours, sweet Shylocket," Richard replied, getting into the spirit of the thing. "Take it and do with it what you will."

"All right." Kempe removed the dagger, which he had hidden in his sleeve, and fell to the ground, dragging Richard down with him. He then gleefully pantomimed cutting out Richard's heart. After the deed was done, he removed the red scarf from Richard's doublet and crumpled it into a ball. Gazing at the scarf, as though it was a heart, Kempe said, "Let me see, should I wear this heart on my bonnet or my sleeve?"

"Oh, Shylocket! Hello!" Richard called out, since Kempe still had him pinned to the floor.

"Antonio!" Kempe exclaimed with mock horror. "Why do you look so pale?"

"Without my heart, I die."

Kempe looked from the "heart" to Richard's dying body. "Now why didn't I think of that before?"

Richard again tried to escape from Kempe's grip, hoping the "play" was now over, but Kempe pushed him back down. "Don't move—dear, dead Antonio," he said, stressing the word "dead" for his squirming co-actor. "I follow you to the grave. But before I do, I have my final speech to say—and it's a long one!"

Kempe collapsed onto the ground, roaring with laughter at his own joke. Richard was laughing, as well. In fact, the entire company was cheering and applauding. Only William looked unhappy.

"Don't look so offended, William," said the clown, as he yanked off the wig and threw it at William. "It was just a joke, a *Jest in Shoreditch*."

Richard had risen, as well, and was brushing the dust off his doublet. But when he saw William start to angrily crumple the wig in his hands—wigs were expensive and he wasn't about to let anyone destroy one—he walked over to William and retrieved it. "This isn't the first time we've asked you to rewrite a few scenes," he reminded his playwright. "Just be grateful we haven't sent your play to the Censor's office. Otherwise, we'd all be in big trouble."

"But you have, Mr. Burbage," said a voice that came from one of the darkened galleries, where the spectators usually sat. "And you are."

Richard Burbage, along with everyone else on the stage, nervously peered into the darkness. Slowly there emerged from the shadows a face, which belonged to Robert Devereux, Earl of Essex. The Earl, who was dressed in a sumptuous attire of black velvet chased with silver threads, made his way unhurriedly to the stage. He was followed by his usual retinue of soldiers and secret agents.

As the company grew near, Richard frantically whispered to his father, "How?"

James Burbage sorrowfully shook his head. "I sent the play off without reading it. I never dreamed that William would write a play like this."

Essex, who had reached the playing area, had overheard the last comment. He walked over to William and said, "I must confess, Mr. Shakespeare, I share the confusion of your colleagues."

"I'm sorry if my play has displeased you, my lord."

"Displeased is not the word. The Censor's office is in shock. People are beginning to talk about you, Mr. Shakespeare. They're starting to say you must be a Catholic. Or worse."

James Burbage, who had been looking faint, returned to life. "A Catholic? In my theatre? William, take your filthy play and get out of here at once!"

"Mr. Burbage, you mistake my words," said Essex. "I didn't say that Mr. Shakespeare *is* a Catholic. Yet."

"Then you don't want me to banish him, my lord?"

"Banish one of the Queen's favorite playwrights? Good heavens, no. It's true that this latest play of his is most troubling, but we must find a way to gently show him the error of his ways."

"Thank you, my lord," said James Burbage. "I'd hate to lose him. He's the most profitable playwright we have."

"I'm sure he is useful. But Mr. Shakespeare, you're looking pale. Have you been eating properly? What sort of salary do you receive for your work?"

"He receives ten percent of The Theatre's profits, my lord," said James Burbage, "just like ..."

"Ten percent? For a favorite of the Queen?" Essex exclaimed with mocking surprise.

"I assure you, my lord," said William, "I am quite satisfied with the arrangement."

"But I am not. No, I must find you a comfortable house, and set you up with a respectable income, and draw up a charming coat of arms for that charming family of yours in Stratford. I warn you, Mr. Shakespeare, I have you in my web. I'll turn you into a gentleman, yet."

When William didn't respond, James Burbage leapt into the breach and said, "Don't be shy, William. Thank the Earl of Essex for his most generous offer."

"It's not every playwright who has the Earl of Essex as his patron," said Richard, glaring in William's direction.

When William still didn't respond, except to stare at Essex with undisguised hatred, Richard moved in front of William and said to Essex, "My lord, please forgive him. It's the strain. William has been working very hard lately and ... and ..."

"He's gone mad," said Kempe, trying to help out.

"That's right. He's gone mad, from the strain," said Richard. "We're hoping it's only temporary."

"Not the most plausible of explanations," said Essex, "but it will do. And now I would like to speak with your madman, in private."

"Oh, my lord, do you think that's wise?" asked James Burbage. "If William should turn violent ..."

"Tut, tut, Mr. Burbage, I have no more fear of mad playwrights than I have of monkeys and Jews. Where can we go?" Essex made a show of looking about the theatre. He then cast his glance upward, to the upper level of the playing area. "Is that heaven I spy? Come, Mr. Shakespeare, we'll have our talk up there, with the angels."

Essex motioned for William to begin the ascent to the upper level, the playing area where sound and light effects such as thunder and lightning were made. Knowing he had no choice, William quickly strode across the stage and exited through a door at the back, which led to a staircase. Before he did the same, Essex assumed an air of concern and said to James Burbage, "If your playwright is temporarily insane, someone will have to take his place and be in charge of rewriting the play."

"Of course, my lord. We'll have a company meeting right now and get to work."

"Excellent, Mr. Burbage. Then I leave it in your capable and responsible hands."

"Responsible, my lord?"

"You are the owner of this theatre."

While the Earl of Essex retreated to "heaven," James Burbage collapsed into a chair.

CHAPTER XV

William could not think why the Earl of Essex hadn't just tossed him into a wagon and carted him off to the Tower, like the others involved in the Lopez plot, for how else could the conversation end? When Essex entered the room, he was even more confused. The Earl of Essex had brought with him a small case, which he now opened. A bottle of wine and two glasses were soon sitting on a dusty table, and the nobleman invited the playwright to take a seat and join him for a friendly glass of wine. William accepted the invitation, albeit reluctantly.

"Some of my men were in Stratford a few weeks ago," said Essex. "It's a lovely town, from what I hear."

"I like it."

"It's a pity about your father. It's always sad to see a man in decline. John Shakespeare is your father, is he not?"

"Yes."

"But your wife Anne and your three children must bring you pleasure."

"Is it a crime for a man to have a family, my lord?" asked William, who found it distasteful to discuss his family with a person he despised.

"On the contrary. It's good to have family and connections, even if they are ... Catholics."

"Surely you don't suspect my aged father or my young son of plotting to murder our sovereign."

"You fascinate me, William."

"In what way, my lord?"

"If I were an ambitious young playwright from a well-known Catholic family, which has seen a member of that family executed for plotting to kill the Queen, I don't know if I'd have had the nerve to write a play like your *Jest in Venice*. Aren't you afraid that the Queen's good opinion of you will change if she ever learns the truth about who you really are?"

"I am a loyal Protestant and subject of the Queen."

"And I can't tell you how relieved I am to hear it." Essex finished the wine in his glass and poured out another. When he saw that William's glass was still full, he said, "You're not drinking, Mr. Shakespeare. I haven't dragged you up here to poison you."

"May I ask why we are here, my lord?"

"I would like to be frank with you, William, and it would help matters if you would stop acting like a five-year-old child whose favorite toy has gotten smashed. You must have known that this play of yours would never pass the Censors, not when I'm trying to get Lopez hanged."

"I didn't know the Censor's office was under your command."

"And now you do. So let's get down to business. You may not realize it, but we have many things in common. We're both intelligent, talented, and ambitious young men — and we're both in trouble."

"You?"

"The Queen is angry at me for arresting Lopez and forcing him to confess."

"Then you don't have proof?"

"I have proof, just not the kind of proof I need to get Lopez convicted."

"Why don't you drop the charges?"

"And look like a fool? That's exactly what William and Robert Cecil would like."

"But surely, my lord, you wouldn't sentence to death an innocent man just to advance your career?"

"Why not?"

When William was silent, Essex continued, "Stop playacting at being shocked about court politics, William.

You're too smart to be that stupid. I don't know why you wrote the play that you did—I assume it was at the instigation of some girl—but whoever she is, forget about her. You're working for me now, do you understand?"

"You assume too much, my lord."

"And you assume too little."

Essex dragged William to the window that looked down upon the stage. The company had recovered from their initial shock. The Burbages and Kempe were seated at a table, where they seemed to be discussing the new play, whose pages were scattered about them. In a different area, some of the actors were playing at dice, laughing and joking. One of the younger actors, who played some of the women's roles, was trying to teach the dog Crab how to walk on his hind legs.

"It's a little world," Essex was saying to William, "a little world filled with little people. Most people strut across the stage of life for a few brief moments and then it's over. With their exit they take with them all memory of their existence. Only a few mortal men are given the gift of eternal remembrance, William, only a few—and you, with your talent, could be one of them. You were meant for greatness, wealth, adulation. Don't throw it all away for an old Jew. You might think a noble gesture will bring you glory, but it's only storybook heroes who live on forever. Real people who try to be heroic end up in some dark, disgusting prison cell, where no one hears their cries. When they die, no one remembers their names."

"Are you threatening me, my lord?"

"Not with the Tower. I can't risk further displeasing the Queen by locking up yet another one of her favorites. But must we speak about threats? All I am asking you to do is to help me, by making a few changes in your play. I need a play that will stir up the mob, rouse their passions, make them demand blood and revenge. I need them to leave the theatre screaming for the death of the Jew so loudly that everyone in London will hear it—including our most gracious sovereign, whose life I am supposedly trying to save. With the public on my side the scales of justice will have to tilt in my favor. The court of law will convict Lopez and the Queen will have no choice—she'll have to sign his death warrant. And after she's done drying her tears for her old, dead Jew, she'll remember her young, living Essex and how he makes her laugh. I'll remember my friends, too. Don't worry, William, I'm not going to forget about you."

"And if I refuse?"

"Remember what happened to Marlowe."

"I thought Christopher Marlowe was accidently murdered during a drunken brawl."

"You young men and your gay escapades—these sorts of accidents are always so tragic. And they happen more frequently than you might suppose. A fight in a tavern with a stranger that spins out of control, a case of mistaken identity on a dark night that ends with a dagger in the back—the streets of London are so dangerous. And it's not much of a life to never know when or where the fatal blow will fall."

Essex paused to watch the action down on the stage. Kempe was amusing the Burbages and some of the actors with his antics. The sound of their laughter was muted, but it could be heard. Essex smiled to see them, like a fond father who is amused by the games of his children.

"See, William, you're already forgotten. They're already rewriting your play."

William did see, and the sight made him wince.

"I'm not saying that your name will be totally forgotten. You are the author of *Romeo and Juliet*, and that Verona play, and *Titus* whatever his name was. But when I think of all the plays that will never be written, and that when people speak about our age and its literary achievements, as they surely will, they will speak of you—who should have been the first name on their's lips—as being a playwright who was only almost as good as Henry Chettle."

Essex glanced over at William, whose eyes were still riveted on the scene below.

"Don't give me your decision now, William. Take your time to think it over. But no matter what you decide, know that your play is going to be rewritten, so that it suits my purpose. And if you do decide to accept my offer, remember to send me the bill when you buy that new house in Stratford. Since your relatives are Catholics, you'll need an extra room for your "secret" chapel," but I won't quibble over the extra expense. And stop looking so worried, William. Your secret is safe with me, as long as our little secret talk today is safe with you."

Essex left. A few minutes later William watched him enter the stage and walk over to the table where the Burbages and Kempe were huddled over the play.

"I see you are all hard at work," Essex called out with a surprisingly strong voice for a nonprofessional actor, but then William, who rightly supposed the performance was for his benefit, recalled that the Earl of Essex was a soldier and had probably learned on the battlefield how to make his voice heard.

"Your command is our ... our ..." once again James Burbage, who was anxious to find out how Essex's interview with William had gone, was uncharacteristically at a loss for words.

"Pleasure?" said Essex, smiling broadly.

"That's exactly the word I was looking for, my lord," said a relieved James Burbage. "If you weren't so busy protecting our Queen and country, I'd suggest you try your hand at writing a play. You do have a way with words, if I may be so bold to say so, my lord."

"I appreciate your frankness and your honesty, Mr. Burbage," said Essex. "In fact, I do have a few ideas for how to improve this play, if I, a mere amateur, may be so bold as to express them."

"We would be honored. Wouldn't we, everyone?"

James Burbage signaled for the entire company to applaud, and the entire company applauded. Another chair was brought to the table, and Essex sat down.

"Let's start with the trial scene. I'm concerned about that speech about mercy. How does it go?"

"The quality of mercy speech?" asked Richard, shuffling through the pages to find it.

"If it displeases you, my lord, we'll cut it right out," said James Burbage.

"You mustn't do that," said Essex, glancing heavenward, where William was still standing at the window. "In my opinion it's one of the finest speeches Mr. Shakespeare has ever written."

"That's exactly what I told the company before you came," said James Burbage. "That speech is a gem, a real gem."

"An apt metaphor for the speech—but what an unworthy vessel it is set in. I couldn't believe my eyes when I saw it had been given to the Jew. "

"It was the strain, my lord," said Richard.

"The madness," Kempe added.

"The madness—I understand," said Essex. "But, of course, everyone sitting here understands that the audience would never want to have compassion for a Jew."

"Of course not," said James Burbage.

"And they would never want to see him pardoned, instead of sentenced to death."

"Never!"

"So who should we give the speech to? The Duke wouldn't say it to himself, and neither Antonio nor Bassanio would plead the Jew's cause. "

"Portia," said Richard, "we'll give the speech to her."

"She's not in the trial scene," James Burbage protested. "There's only the Duke and the Jew and the lawyers and ..."

"Have her be one of the lawyers."

"A lady can't be a lawyer."

"Yes, she can, Father," said Richard. "We'll have her dressed up as a man."

"Like in *Two Gentlemen of Verona*?" said Kempe. "The audience loved that."

"Then that problem is solved," said Essex, "and solved well, I might add."

James Burbage was about to say something flattering, but Essex was already continuing on to the next problem. "I must confess, Mr. Burbage, that I am shocked that you chose a noble actor like your son — who has portrayed a king of England — to play the role of Shylock."

"Well, it was Richard III that he played, my lord."

"Yes, but when I think of a Jew, I have a very different image in my mind. I hope you're not offended, Mr. Burbage."

"Not in the least, my lord," said Richard, bowing slightly.

"Does his lordship perhaps have some other actor in mind for the part?" asked James Burbage.

"As a matter of fact, I do. Could I ask your company to form a semi-circle in the center of the stage?"

James Burbage sprang into action, and within moments the entire company was in place. Essex, who had asked for the skullcap that Richard had been wearing and received it, slowly made his way around the half-circle, sometimes pausing before an actor and sometimes continuing on without making a stop. When he reached Will Kempe, he raised the skullcap high in the air and then crowned the clown with the hat, to Kempe's extreme delight.

While Kempe began to gleefully cavort about the stage, Essex glanced heavenward, to where William was still standing at the window.

"I leave the rest to you," Essex called out to the Burbages. Then, his purpose accomplished, he made his exit, followed by his attendants.

CHAPTER XVI

The rack was one of the most feared instruments of torture in those days. Sometimes just the sight of the wooden frame and its chains and pulleys was enough to make a prisoner talk. Other times, the prisoner was placed in a nearby room, where he was forced to listen to a co-conspirator being tortured, and the sound of those agonized screams coming from another made him open his own mouth and reveal whatever information he knew.

The actual placement of a prisoner on that hellish bed was usually used only as a last resort, since an English court could be squeamish about accepting a confession uttered under those conditions; the judges knew that when a body was stretched to the breaking point, the truth could be stretched along with it.

Of course, often the judges had to set aside their personal feelings and were forced to accept such testimony as valid. Preserving the life of the Queen was the State's first priority, and the thinking was that it was better to execute ten innocent men by mistake than to allow one guilty man to go free and continue to pursue his plots. But the court preferred, even if it was all a pretense, that the damning evidence be found some other way.

It was therefore something of an art to be a successful interrogator. One had to know a great deal about human nature and what made a person tick. Fear was only one of several motivators. Money, of course, was another. But the Earl of Essex was justifiably proud of the piece of work he had done in The Theatre that day, because he knew that the torture he had devised for the playwright William Shakespeare was, in its own way, a work of art. Indeed, after Essex left The Theatre and rode away, he was quite certain that his prisoner, although not in chains, was still rooted to the spot in that airy tower, right where he had left him, gazing down with horror at the sight of the utter annihilation of his play.

And he was right.

William was still too much in shock to be able to analyze and put into words what he was feeling. That he had been beaten, he had no doubt. Without the backing of his theatre company, his play, as he had written it, was useless as a defense for the Jewish physician. In theory, he could have sent the manuscript to the Queen, but there was no guarantee that she would read it. The more likely scenario was that it would be intercepted by either the agents of Essex or the agents of the Cecils and therefore it would never reach the Queen's hands.

His attempt at playing a hero's part had been thwarted, as well. If he had been taken to the Tower — and from there to the gallows — he could have made some rousing final speech that would have comforted his parents and filled his wife and children with pride. But if his silent lifeless body were to be found in some dark alley, a supposed victim of a drunken brawl, what comfort would there be then? He would have only added more shame to his family's already heavy burden.

To be honest, though, it was not his flesh-and-blood family that was on William's mind at that moment. It was the thought that his work — the deepest expression of his soul, the child of his imagination — was being reduced to a mockery of its former and truer self, courtesy of the jerky, jigging, jack-in-the-box gyrations of the clown William Kempe.

Kempe had wasted no time in getting "into" his role, which for him meant getting into the traditional costume of the stage Jew — a red wig and beard for his head and face, and a long black caftan for his twitching body. As he danced and drooled about the stage, with a long drawn dagger completing his costume, not a single shred remained of the carefully drawn portrait of the dignified, long-suffering Jew that William had so painstakingly constructed.

It was torture to watch. The comment is not meant to denigrate the very real physical pain that so many human beings have been forced to endure, throughout the ages, at the hands of their tormentors. But for an artist like Shakespeare, the pain of watching his play being destroyed—and with it his reputation, his ambitions, his dreams—was physical. He could feel the chambers of his brain cracking and keeling, until he felt he could no longer bear the strain.

Meanwhile, down below, on the playing area, Kempe called out to Richard, who was still sitting with his father and looking over the manuscript. "Antonio, come here for a minute. Antonio! Richard, I'm calling you!"

"What?"

"I want to try out some business in the pound of flesh scene."

"So get Antonio."

"You are Antonio now."

"Sorry, I forgot."

Richard joined Kempe, as did the actor playing Bassanio. After the two actors were placed where Kempe wanted them to stand, the clown said to Richard, "Give me the last line of your speech."

"I don't know what it is. I left the page on the table." He looked about the stage area and called out, "Prompter! Get me the speech."

The prompter, who sometimes was cast as Kempe's comic foil and therefore had learned to be quick or risk getting a kick in the shin, ran to the table and then to Richard in record time.

Richard found the place and began to read, "*But lend it rather to thine enemy, who if he break, thou mayst with better face exact the penalty.*"

"*Why, look you, how you storm!*" said Kempe as Shylock, enjoying himself immensely as he turned his face into a "storm" of grimaces. "*I would be friends with you and have your love. Forget the shames that you have stained me with. Supply your wants, and take no doit of usance for my moneys, and you'll not hear me. This is kind I offer.*" The clown then turned to the "audience" and, in an aside, gave a comically evil laugh.

"*This were kindness,*" said Bassanio.

Kempe, who was still trying out various demonic laughs, missed his cue. Richard therefore said to him, "You can work on that later. If you need me for something, let's get on with it."

Kempe gave one last laugh, and then continued with the scene. "*This kindness will I show. Go with me to the notary, seal me there your single bond; and, in merry sport, if you repay me not on such a day and in such a place, such sum or sums as are expressed in the condition, let the forfeit be nominated for an equal pound of your fair flesh to be cut off and taken in what part of your body pleaseth me.*"

"*Content, in faith, I'll seal to such a bond,*" said Richard as Antonio.

While "Antonio" and "Bassanio" continued with their lines, Kempe turned to the audience again and removed the stage dagger from his cloak. With a crazed look in his eye and a wicked smile on his face, he pantomimed sharpening the dagger. Then he approached Richard from behind and began to act out, with ludicrously exaggerated movements, exactly how he was going to cut out the pound of flesh from the unsuspecting Antonio.

While Kempe's fellow thespians roared with laughter, William rushed down the backstage staircase and entered upon the stage. Grabbing the dagger from Kempe's hand, he said, "What do you think you're doing?"

"I'm acting."

"You call that grotesque buffoonery acting?"

"This is a rehearsal, William," said Richard. "Kempe is allowed to take an artistic risk."

"That's right, Mr. Iambic Pentameter," said Kempe. "You ought to be grateful that you have William Kempe to liven up your plays."

"If you want me to rewrite this play," William said to Richard, "tell Kempe to tone it down."

Richard made a show of considering the proposition. "Do I understand you correctly, William? You're willing to rewrite the play, according to the instructions of the Earl of Essex?"

"Yes, if you'll stop Kempe from drooling all over the stage."

"The audience will expect to see a knife," said Richard.

"He can do some comic business when he sharpens his knife during the trial scene. But Shylock has to be at least semi-human in the beginning scenes, otherwise there's no drama. There's no play."

"If you were any other playwright, I'd let you hang yourself, after the stunt you pulled with this *Jest* of yours," said Richard. "But you're too valuable to The Theatre to waste on a one-time performance at a public execution." He then turned to Kempe and said, "Tone it down."

Kempe wasn't happy, but he agreed to try—but not before he made a parting show of stabbing William in the back.

ii.

William locked himself in his rooms to rewrite his play; Richard Burbage made sure of that. The new play that he wrote wasn't a masterpiece, but it would pass muster. The only problem, as it so often is in the theatre, was the final scene. The Earl of Essex, as well as his theatre company, was expecting a rousing finale. Just as the Jew must be executed in real life, the Jew must be executed on the stage. But how to do it, that was the question?

"Why not burn him at the stake?" Kempe suggested, after William brought the unfinished manuscript to The Theatre and the parts were copied.

"Oh, no, not another fire on stage," said Richard. "I suppose we could hack him to pieces, like it was a real execution."

"Too bloody," said John Burbage. "You know how hard it is to get fake blood out of the costumes."

"I don't see why we can't have a boiling cauldron," said Kempe. "I could do something very funny with that."

"We can't do the same thing that Marlowe did," said William, who had been listening glumly while the others were talking.

"We could fill ours with hot oil, instead of water," said Kempe.

"That's an idea," said John Burbage. "If you can't think of anything better, we'll have to go with that. In the meantime, let's start rehearsing the other new scenes."

iii.

At Guildhall a different discussion was taking place. The trial of Dr. Lopez had begun, and the Earl of Essex had gone all out to make sure the trial would be a show talked about all over London. The usually small tribunal had been expanded to fifteen worthies, resplendent in their ruffs and robes, who sat in judgment above the accused man. The conclusion of the trial was known to all—an indicted man like Dr. Lopez must be convicted, for in those days to be indicted was to already be guilty of the crime. But what was not yet known was that Essex, too, was going to have last-act trouble.

The trial didn't take long. Dr. Lopez continued to insist that the poisoning plot had been, in truth, a plot to trick the Spanish king, and that he had confessed only to evade being tortured on the rack. But his haggard face and haunted eyes all too clearly revealed that he knew the game was up; neither the judges nor the jury were listening.

From time to time the physician would try to catch the eye of the Cecils, father and son. He was one of the few people in the room who knew that he had served William Cecil in the capacity of translator during Cecil's attempts to broker a secret peace agreement with King Philip. But if he thought that the elder Cecil might still come to his aid because of that earlier connection, he saw that hope extinguished when he learned of the new revelations that had gushed out of the mouths of the Portuguese prisoners tortured in the Tower. A new name had been added to the list of double agents: Manuel de Andrada.

Andrada, a Portuguese spy who had been the principal go-between during the peace negotiations, had turned out to be one of King Philip's loyal agents. That was a double embarrassment for William Cecil; not only had his attempts to negotiate a peace treaty failed, but he had allowed himself to be tricked by the Spanish king and his Portuguese spy. And since it is always easier to blame someone else for one's failings, Cecil decided to blame Dr. Lopez, whom Cecil decided must have played a contributing role in the fiasco, pretending to be a loyal subject and servant even while he was secretly plotting against England and betraying her secrets to the enemy.

Perhaps Cecil was entitled to have his suspicions. Obviously, he knew that Lopez was a spy—he, himself, had employed the physician to work on behalf of English interests. But Cecil had been unaware of the work Lopez had done for Walsingham—the supposed plots to poison Don Antonio and the Queen—since each politician worked separately and often jealously guarded his own secrets.

This new revelation about Andrada made Cecil wonder about what else the physician might be hiding, what other embarrassing plots might come to light. From there it wasn't difficult to become convinced that even if Essex was wrong about the plot to poison the Queen, he was right in a general sense: Rodrigo Lopez was a dangerous man, much too dangerous to let live.

It therefore took the court only a few hours to decide that Dr. Lopez was guilty of plotting to assassinate the Queen.

This should have been a day of triumph for Essex. He had proved that his "mare's nest" had been a true and dangerous plot against the Queen. He had beaten the Cecils, and forced them to come over to his side. All that was lacking to complete his victory was the death warrant signed by the Queen's hand, which was usually quick in coming. But it did not come.

Ferreira and Tinoco were also tried and convicted. The Tower had practically become a Portuguese colony. And still the death warrant did not come.

Essex was not about to let the matter drop. If he could not force the Queen's hand, he could fan the fires of hatred against Spain and the Jew who had been hired by the Spanish king, to remind the Queen of where the passions of her people lay. He therefore hired a few writers to dash off some ditties to be sung in the taverns. And he sent off a hasty message to The Theatre: "Where's the play?"

CHAPTER XVII

John Burbage was doing what he enjoyed doing the most: counting the proceeds from that day's performance. The shiny coins made a lovely heap of towers on his table, since The Theatre's latest production, *The Merchant of Venice*, was a rousing success. Even more importantly, the Earl of Essex loved the play. He had seen it several times, each time bringing a large party of friends and hangers-on to see it and be seen. There was also a rumor that Essex was paying regular folk—common laborers, and the like—to attend the play and stir up the audience at the right moments, but John Burbage didn't care. The important thing was that the play was a hit; how the pit was filled wasn't his concern.

William also watched the performances more often than was his wont, but he was less elated by the full houses. He wasn't privy to court secrets and so he didn't know why the Queen was refusing to sign the death warrant. He only knew that he wished the Lopez story would end, in one way or the other.

He was not alone. Both Essex and William Cecil wanted the execution to take place, and it was annoying that the Queen had interfered and instructed the Tower's lieutenant to ignore any attempts by the Privy Council to go ahead with the job. Why, no one knew. Elizabeth had her secrets, as well. She might have believed, in her heart, her physician was loyal, and so she didn't want to spill innocent blood. Or she might have been guided by political considerations. Dr. Lopez had rich and influential relatives in Constantinople. Just two years earlier she had used them to try to convince the Ottoman Sultan to become her ally in England's fight against Spain. The alliance had not come to fruition, but perhaps she was in no rush to turn her friends in the Levant into enemies.

In the end, Cecil bypassed the Queen by having Dr. Lopez removed from the Tower—and the Queen's protection—and taken to another prison, where he was given a second "trial." This time, there would be no delay between sentence and execution, and a messenger boy rushed into The Theater to tell John Burbage the news.

"Sssh! There's a performance going on," said John Burbage.

"But it's about Dr. Lopez," said the child.

"Well? What about him?"

"The execution is going to be tomorrow. They say he's going to be hanged first, and then drawn and quartered. And then they're going to throw his body to the dogs."

John Burbage removed a coin from the pile and placed it into the child's outstretched hand; news like this deserved a reward. He then decided that he must make a speech at the end of the performance, and so he went into the theatre to wait.

William was standing in the back, watching the performance, which was nearing its conclusion. "We've done it!" John Burbage whispered excitedly. "The execution is set for tomorrow."

William didn't reply, but there was no need to. John Burbage's eyes were already on the players, entranced by the trial scene that was then taking place on the stage.

"*A pound of that same merchant's flesh is thine. The court awards it, and the law doth give it,*" said "Portia," who was dressed in her lawyer's robes, to the delight of the audience.

"*Most rightful judge!*" said Kempe as Shylock, doing a little hopping jig to express his glee, which was rewarded by a short burst of laughter.

"*And you must cut this flesh from off his breast. The law allows it, and the court awards it.*"

The little jig turned into a full-fledged dance, complete with wild waving of his knife as Kempe shouted, "*Most learned judge! A sentence! Come prepare!*"

"*Tarry a little; there's something else,*" said "Portia," moving to the center of the stage. "*This bond doth give thee here no jot of blood. The words expressly are 'a pound of flesh.' Take then, thy bond, take thou thy pound of flesh. But in the cutting of it if thou dost shed one drop of Christian blood, thou diest, and all thy goods are confiscate.*"

The crowd began to murmur its approval as the actor playing Bassanio said, "*O upright judge! Mark, Jew. O learned judge.*"

Kempe, caught with his dagger in mid-air, asked, with dumb amazement, "*Is that the law?*"

"*Thyself shalt see the act,*" replied the actor playing Portia. "*For as thou urgest justice, be assured thou shalt have justice more than thou desir'st.*"

At that point, several stagehands hauled onto the stage a ridiculously large cauldron, and the crowd cheered its entrance.

Kempe, shriveled and sniveling as he made a great show of being terrified by the cauldron, begged, "*I pray you, give me leave to go from hence. I am not well.*"

As if on cue, several members of the audience began to heckle him.

"*Down, Jew, and beg for mercy of the Duke.*"

Kempe turned from "Portia" to the actor playing the "Duke" and fell to his knees. "*I beseech you, wrest once the law to your authority. To do a great right, do a little wrong.*"

"*Shylock, thou shalt soon see the difference of our spirit,*" the "Duke" thundered. "*Thy wealth being forfeit to the state, thou hast not left the value of a cord. Even so, thou wilt die at the state's expense.*"

Various actors, dressed as judges, escorted Kempe to the platform where the cauldron was "bubbling" away, while the crowd continued to laugh and cheer. One of the actors attached a rope and pulley mechanism to Kempe, which hauled him upwards and began to swing him back and forth over the cauldron, before dunking him inside it—repeating the stage business several times.

Kempe, who was in theatre heaven, made a great show of being frightened to death, wiggling his legs madly to avoid being scalded when he was lowered into the cauldron, and pumping his legs wildly, as though trying to run away, when he was suspended in the air.

Then the rope was lowered and he was dumped, for the last time, into the cauldron, and he disappeared.

The mob roared.

ii.

On June 7, 1594, there was a performance in London that no theatre could rival: the execution of Dr. Lopez.

The physician, as well as Ferreira and Tinoco, were carted through that city's streets to Tyburn, where a hangman was waiting for them. The route took the condemned men through Holborn, presumably so that Dr. Lopez could take one last tortured look at his home. If his wife and children were looking through a window to say a silent, last goodbye, or if they had remained inside to spare the physician his final shame, we do not know. But we do know that there was nothing glorious about that last journey. The open cart was accompanied by the taunts and jeers of a jolly crowd determined to enjoy their morning's fun. Perhaps it was a spontaneous gathering, or perhaps some members of the crowd were in the Earl of Essex's pay, hired to stir up the mob to a frenzied pitch at this real performance, just as they had done at The Theatre.

But whether it was spontaneous or staged, Richard Burbage was right when he shouted to Kempe, "What a show!"

"That Earl of Essex knows how to give the dogs a bone," Kempe happily agreed.

Dr. Lopez was the first of the three prisoners to be led up to the platform. After the noose was placed about his neck, an official read out, "Rodrigo Lopez, judgment has been passed against you, with the applause of all the world. Have you anything to say?"

"I am innocent. I love the Queen as much as I love Jesus Christ."

"And just how much is that, Jew?" someone shouted out, and the mob laughed.

It is tempting to see the physician's exit line as pathetic, the ineffectual protest of a broken man grabbing at a feeble straw. Surely, he must have known that no one in that pit of rowdy, blood-thirsty humanity would have been persuaded by his words and shown him mercy at the last moment. It is also odd that he, himself, made mention of his checkered religious past; it wasn't a court of the Spanish Inquisition that had tried him and found him guilty of a religious crime, and so a protestation that he was a loyal Christian could not help his English civil case. Had the strain of the last several months made him mad?

Or had the last sight of his home made him maddeningly sane, and therefore determined to salvage whatever he could of his shattered position and fortune for those he was leaving behind—his wife and children? Were his last words directed not to the ignorant crowd, but to someone who would understand the language of secret code in which they were spoken, namely his sovereign, Queen Elizabeth?

We think so. When Dr. Lopez declared that he loved her as much as he loved the Christian deity, she should have understood, like everyone else, that on the surface he was saying that he didn't love her at all— which was an insult, an open defiance, and even a treasonous statement

Yet as later developments were to prove, Elizabeth heard and understood something very different.

Elizabeth had begun her reign by displaying tolerance toward her Catholic subjects. That ended when political developments on the Continent turned Europe into a jousting tournament between Protestant and Catholic warring sides, and the conflict spilled into England. Several failed plots to kill her and put a Catholic monarch on the throne, in her place, dampened her youthful proclivity to live and let live. But she didn't go far enough in her Religious Settlement to suit some of her more extremist Protestant subjects. She therefore spent most of her reign being too Protestant for the Catholics and not Protestant enough for the Puritans, and watching her back when in the presence of both of them—which might have made her sympathetic to the balancing act of her Jewish-Protestant physician, who was too Christian for the Jews and too Jewish for the Christians.

It also might have made her appreciate the physician for the rarity that he was, during those times: an Englishman first. Unlike so many of her subjects, whose love for her—and their loyalty—was contingent upon how she played the religious-political game and whom she favored, she knew that the tension between Protestants and Catholics wasn't his battle; as a Jew he lost, no matter what kind of Christian sat on the throne.

She therefore perhaps heard, in the physician's veiled language of political intrigue and heightened speech of the stage: I don't love the Christian deity and I don't love Christian kings and queens. I am loyal to you, Elizabeth, because you are an English monarch who rules according to English civil law. I am loyal to you because it is in your land that my family has found a safe haven in the past—and can expect to be treated fairly in the future.

iii.

William had not gone to the execution. But he almost felt as if he had. It was the topic of conversation everywhere— backstage at The Theatre, in the public houses, he couldn't even go to the fishmonger's without being treated to a detailed description of the physician's grisly demise. He listened but could not join in with the laughter. Instead, he wandered about London like a pathetic malcontent who looked upon the riotous party that was taking place—with its celebration of all that was vicious and cruel, its freedom from all refinement and restraint—like a dour-faced Puritan. Even the Earl of Essex commented that he was acting like a full-fledged Protestant, at last.

He couldn't bear to watch the performance of his play, but he couldn't bear to stay away from The Theatre, either. He therefore hung about behind the stage, getting in the way of the actors and stagehands and in other ways making himself a nuisance. After the performance, when everyone else had gone home, he would ascend to the playing area to think, and wait.

One day, when the afternoon light was fading to dusk, he thought he heard the sound of footsteps moving about in the stalls. He usually wasn't superstitious, nor was he prone to seeing demons and goblins in the dark corners of his room or cupboards, but this wasn't a usual time in his life. He supposed that it wasn't entirely implausible that the soul of the dead physician might make a trip to The Theatre, to point an accusing finger.

But when two figures emerged from the shadows, neither one of them had the guise of the doctor. Instead, William recognized the faces of his childhood friends, Henry and Joan Rivers. He also saw that they were dressed for traveling.

"You are leaving England?" he asked, when they had joined him on the stage.

"We are going to Constantinople," said Henry. "Dr. Lopez had family there, and there we will be able to live openly as Jews."

"I wish you good luck."

"Thank you, William."

There was an awkward pause, and then William said, "Well, aren't you going to rant at me, call me a traitor and a coward and a conniving knave who was willing to sell his soul to the Earl of Essex to save his own earthly neck?"

"I was going to ask you why you did it," said Henry. "But now there's no need. I'll just say goodbye."

Henry motioned to his sister to leave.

"Wait!" William called after them. "I gave you my blessing. Can you not forgive me and give me your blessing in return?"

Henry was about to speak, when Joan stopped him. She walked over to William and studied him for a moment. "You want a blessing from us, after you killed off one of your stage Jews and turned the other one, your Jessica, into a Christian?"

"Joan," Henry said, "it's a long way to the port. We should go."

"My blessing to Mr. Shakespeare won't take long, Henry, although I hope it will last him for eternity."

"Your brother is right, Joan," said William, turning his eyes away, so as not to meet hers. "The light is fading. Soon it will be night."

"And then it will be morning, for some of us. But for others it will still be night. Yes, I do have a blessing for you. I bless you that your plays will be remembered but that you, the man William Shakespeare—your life, your loves, your lofty thoughts and your lowly fears, your very best deeds and your very worst failings—will disappear, as though you had no more substance than the characters you created for your precious stage. I bless you that people will think you a poacher, a hostler, an uneducated boor or, conversely, a nobleman of the highest rank, anything but what you really are; and that future generations will insist that your plays were written by another hand, or several hands, perhaps even by a Catholic or a Muslim or a Jewish hand. And, finally, I bless you that when the End of Days are here that God will raise your bones from their dusty grave and restore vision to your hollow eyes so that you will see this: You may humiliate us and boycott us, deny us your honors and write

~ 194 ~

us out of your books; you may banish us and burn us and hack our bodies into a hundred million pieces before your jeering crowds, but you will never win. The Jewish people will never betray their faith. We will always be there, reminding you that there is a God and a Divine moral code that rules the world, and that those who defy that code are doomed to fail and be destroyed by the very traps that they devise for others. You will never silence us, Mr. Shakespeare. We will never disappear."

They left. The light continued to fade; the shadows increased both in number and in depth. That play of light and shadow played tricks with the eyes. And so when another figure emerged from the darkening gloom, William was at first unsure if the person was truly real. But then the man spoke.

"You don't look well, William," said the Earl of Essex. "Truly, I worry about you."

"I am well enough to play my part, my lord."

"I'm glad to hear it, because I have some troubling news."

"More plots against the Queen?"

Essex shook his head. "It seems that Dr. Lopez was innocent, after all. Therefore, our Queen, being a most just and gracious sovereign, has graciously agreed to compensate the doctor's family for their loss. They shall retain title to their goods and property — something they would not be able to do, if the Queen believed that Dr. Lopez had betrayed her. Her Majesty has retained only one small token of remembrance, a ring to remind her of her old and faithful Jewish servant."

"A diamond and ruby ring, from the King of Spain?"

"You know it?"

"Yes, and I suppose you would like to know how."

"Some other time; today, we must talk about your play."

"My play?"

"William, I'll be frank with you. The Queen is furious with me for executing Dr. Lopez. And she's not happy with you, either."

"Me?"

"She's let it be known that she's very disappointed by that play of yours."

"*My* play, my lord?"

"Yes, Mr. Shakespeare, your play. It's your name that's on the advertisement, and the Queen is shocked at your callous treatment of the Jew. She thought it was most uncharacteristic of you."

"Perhaps, then, I should start a rumor that it was written by Christopher Marlowe."

"Look, William, this is no time to be quarrelsome. It would be foolish to let this incident jeopardize our careers. So stop moping like a sulky schoolboy and rewrite the play."

"Do you have a suggestion for how I should do it, my lord?"

"Yes, I do. You have to make the Duke more merciful— like our most gracious sovereign, who likes to pretend she is all mercy even when she's cutting off her subjects' heads."

"Anything else?"

"Make the Jew more sympathetic. It was a terrible idea to cast Kempe in the role. I can't think what made you do it. But find someone else, someone with at least a modicum of dignity. And put back in that speech about the Jew having eyes and hair ..."

"Hands, my lord."

"What?"

"*Hath not a Jew eyes? Hath not a Jew hands, organs, dimensions ...*"

"Whatever. But don't put the speech in such a prominent place, like you did the last time. You can't let the Jew beat the Christian during the trial scene. That can never happen. You do understand that, don't you, William? "

"I understand. You want Shylock to be sympathetic, but not too sympathetic."

"Exactly. So have Shylock say the speech to himself, or to a servant, or to someone else who's unimportant. And give the play a happier ending."

"But not too happy?"

"Why not make the Jew a Christian at the end, like his daughter?"

"Do you think I should give him a love interest? Marry him off? Order restored, love conquers all, that sort of thing?"

"You're the playwright, William. I leave it to you. Just get rid of that cauldron!"

The Earl of Essex stormed off, almost bumping into Richard Burbage and William Kempe.

"Gentlemen," said Essex, and then he disappeared into the darkness.

"My lord," said Richard and Kempe, bowing slightly in the direction of the retreating figure. They then joined William on the stage.

"We've come up with an idea for our next play," said Richard.

"I don't know if there's going to be a new play. I belong to the Earl of Essex now, and he might keep me busy rewriting *The Merchant of Venice* for the rest of my life: we like the Jews, we don't like the Jews, we like the Jews, we don't like ..."

"Don't be ridiculous," said Richard. "By this time next year, no one will remember the Lopez incident. Tell him your idea, Kempe."

"It's like this," said Kempe. "There are two sets of lovers, and they have to go into a forest, and then everything gets mixed up, and then everything gets straightened out. The end."

"Is it my imagination," William said to Richard, "or have I heard that plot before?"

"Kempe, you forgot to tell William about the best part," said Richard.

"It's true that Will Kempe will be at the very Bottom of the play, as usual. But I'm sure, Richard, that William will write a nice part for you, too."

"No, tell him about the dream."

"The dream? Oh! Where's my mind? I forgot to tell you what happens in the forest."

"Well, what does happen?" William asked.

"They fall asleep!" said Kempe.

"Who falls asleep?"

"Everybody!"

William looked from Kempe to Richard. "That sounds exciting."

"Kempe, you're not telling it right," said Richard. He then explained to William, "After they go into the forest, everybody falls asleep. And so everything that happens afterward is a dream."

"A dream?"

"A summer night's dream, in the forest; think of all the fun we can have."

"We'll have the King of the Fairies and his crew making mischief," said Kempe, "putting fairy dust in everyone's eyes and mixing everybody up."

"It will be like a spirit of madness has come over the world," said Richard. "The characters will be able to say and do things they'd never be able to do in real life."

"A dream?" said William, considering the idea.

Kempe nodded his head, his eyes already aglow and his ears already hearing the applause. "The audience will love it."

BERLIN

CHAPTER XVIII

Something was pounding and Paul Hoffmann wasn't sure if the noise was coming from outside his family home near the Opernplatz or from inside his head. He also didn't know how long he had been lying on the sofa in his room — if it had been a day or a year — and he was still too groggy to really care. But the noise was irritating, and once he determined that it was coming from outside, he had a thought to go to the open window and shut it.

That was a mistake. The moment he moved his head a wave of pain made him close his eyes and sink back down upon the pillows.

The pain eventually subsided, but it had left him too weak to think about moving. Instead, he lay motionless, listening. He thought he heard footsteps on the stairs, probably a maid going about her work. He also thought he heard the voice of his Grandmama Larissa, although the sound was too muffled for him to distinguish what she was saying.

Then the doorbell rang, and he strained to hear what was going on in the hallway below.

Downstairs, the parlor maid had opened the front door, cautiously. She was not familiar with the three young men who were standing on the front step, since Paul had kept his university life separate from his life at home.

"We're friends of Paul, from the university," Meyer explained, nodding towards Joseph and Franz, who were standing beside him. "Is he well enough yet to receive visitors?"

"The university?" the maid asked, saying the word with the same feeling she might have expressed if they had said they had come from a leper colony.

"Yes."

"I'll have to ask."

The maid closed the door. Joseph took a step backwards to survey the building. "Do think this whole building is Paul's house, or just a floor?"

Meyer signaled to him to be quiet. A moment later the door reopened.

Larissa Hoffmann might have been Paul's grandmother, but the years had been kind to her and she was still a beautiful woman. She was also elegantly dressed, but not overly so—just as her manners were elegant without falling to the extreme of either haughtiness or false friendliness.

"Gentlemen, I'm Paul's grandmother, Frau Hoffmann," she said, taking in the three young men one by one with her smile, even as she appraised their relative wealth and standing in society with her shrewd eyes. "How very kind of you to come."

"May we see Paul?" asked Meyer.

"I'm sorry, but he's still not well enough to have visitors. Perhaps next week he'll be feeling stronger."

"We won't be in Berlin next week."

Larissa Hoffmann raised an eyebrow, but that was the extent of her curiosity, or, at least, as much as she was willing to show. "I shall tell Paul that you called," she said. "Now, if you will excuse me."

Before she could close the door, Meyer removed an envelope from his jacket and said, "Frau Hoffmann, would you please give this letter to Paul? We were quite good friends. I wouldn't want him to think that I left Germany without saying goodbye."

"Very well." She took the letter and closed the door.

The maid had retreated to the drawing room, where she was giving a pane of glass in the front window a vigorous rub. She didn't know what had happened to the scion of the family; she knew only that something had happened. She therefore watched the retreat of the three young men with interest. She also saw one of them—Joseph—turn back to give the Hoffmann mansion another look, shake his head, and say something to the others, who also looked at the house, and then turned away.

"Let me know when the doctor arrives," said Larissa Hoffmann. "I'll be resting in my room."

"Yes, Frau Hoffmann."

"And make sure all the windows are shut tight and the curtains drawn this evening."

"Yes, Frau Hoffmann."

ii.

When Paul saw his grandmother glide past his door, he called out to her. Larissa Hoffmann returned and stood in the doorway. "Did you have a nice rest?"

"Not really."

"More bad dreams?"

"I suppose so. Who was at the door?" He wondered that she did not come into the room and sit, as she usually did when he was awake.

"Some young men," she replied, with the same tone of voice she might have used to say that some workmen had called. "They said they were friends of yours."

"From the university? Why didn't you let them in?" In his excitement, he tried to raise himself to a sitting position. But once again the sudden movement set off a wave of excruciating pain in his head, and he collapsed back down onto the pillows.

"That's why," she said, going over to the sofa. She brushed a wisp of hair off his forehead, and straightened the blanket that had fallen half off. "You know you mustn't do anything that might upset you. Remember what the doctor said."

Paul slowly turned his head toward the window. "What's that pounding noise? Where is it coming from?"

"Does it hurt your head?"

"Yes."

"I'll prepare a headache powder for you."

"No, I don't want to sleep anymore."

"You need to rest." She went over to a table where a variety of bottles and medicine boxes sat, along with a carafe of water and a glass.

"Why won't you tell me what they're doing out there?"

"There's no need to get upset, Paul. It's really nothing. They're building a platform over by the Opernplatz. Apparently there is going to be some sort of ceremony there this evening."

"What sort of ceremony?"

Larissa Hoffmann brought the headache mixture over to Paul. "Drink this."

The mixture was bitter tasting, and he really didn't want to go back to sleep. It felt like he had been sleeping forever. But his grandmother had a will made from steel and she made sure that he drank down the entire glass.

"Now close your eyes and forget about all this unpleasantness," she said. "Shall I read to you? Would you like to hear some Shakespeare? Remember how I used to read the plays to you when you were a child? They always put you straight to sleep."

"I thought I heard something about a letter," said Paul, struggling to keep his eyes open. "Did I receive a letter from the university?"

"The letter was from one of your friends. I'll put it on the table, next to the headache powder. You can read it when you're feeling better."

"Didn't I receive anything from the university? Surely, they must have decided about my thesis by now."

"Darling, do try to put what happened out of your mind. Thinking and fretting about it won't do any good."

"Why don't they write? Or why don't they send someone here to apologize? Isn't that what you said they would do — what they must do? Send someone here, to make a formal apology?"

"I told you yesterday, Paul. Our lawyer has been in contact with the university's administration. They have assured us that what happened to you wasn't at all personal. None of the Jewish students are going to be allowed to graduate."

"None?"

"But do stop worrying. Soon this will all blow over, and Germany will return to her senses. The university will too. In a few months, you'll be sitting in a café with your friends and having a good laugh about all this. Now close your eyes, Paul. You must sleep."

iii.

The platform was finished, and the pounding that had filled the Opernplatz all morning had finally come to an end. But the square was far from quiet. Members of the German Students' Association were busy preparing for the book-burning ceremony scheduled to take place that evening. While some of the students placed Nazi flags in prominent places — including one that was draped over a table that stood in the center of the podium — others were carting mounds of books from the nearby university library. Even dump trucks had been called into service, and Kurt Ellersiek, the Association's leader watched the progress, marked by the ever-rising mound of discarded books, with a satisfied smile.

An official limousine drove into the square. Joseph Goebbels, the Nazi Minister of Propaganda and the "genius" behind the book-burning ceremony concept, alighted from the car and limped over to the platform.

Ellersiek rushed over to greet his distinguished visitor, who was to be the main speaker at the event. The two conferred about the placement of microphones and camera crews and, of course, the bonfire.

When those matters of logistics had been decided, the student leader asked, "A question has come up about the works of William Shakespeare. He does make fun of the German suitor in *The Merchant of Venice*. Should we burn his books, as well?"

Dr. Goebbels laughed. "Don't worry, Herr Ellersiek. Shakespeare's virtues far outweigh his transgressions. By the time I'm through with him, Herr Shakespeare will be one of our most faithful writers."

iv.

The Berlin book-burning ceremony took place on the night of May 10, 1933. Thirty-four university towns in Germany had their own smaller events that same night, while rain forced several other towns to postpone their ceremonies until later in the month or in June. More than 20,000 books were burned. The ceremonies were a rousing success.

That success didn't just happen. Goebbels was an enthusiastic planner, and no detail was considered to be too small to warrant his attention. Bands were enlisted to play their rousing marches, while students mingled with the crowd, enjoining their fellows to join them in patriotic song. For his speech, Goebbels, who was slight in build, made sure that he was surrounded by more sturdily-built men, some of them students dressed in uniform, representing the new Germany. Before him stood a table, and he had made sure beforehand that the Nazi flag draped over that table was placed so that the light illuminated the large swastika in the flag's center. Thus surrounded by symbols of Nazi might and glory, it no longer mattered that just a few years earlier Goebbels had been a failed novelist and playwright. He was now writing the script for the nation to follow, and his show was a rousing success.

"German men and women!" he called out to the crowd, and to the radio microphone that captured his every word and sent those words not only throughout Germany but to the entire world. "The age of arrogant Jewish intellectualism is now at an end."

The newsreel director nudged his cameraman to get a shot of the crowd, who were listening with rapt attention. The camera then panned back to the Minister of Propaganda.

"You are doing the right thing," Goebbels continued, "to consign the unclean spirit of the past to the flames. German students! Consign everything un-German to the fire."

A second cameraman had his lens focused on the bonfire. He motioned for a few students to step up to the fire and toss in their books. The flames responded by leaping up to touch the night sky. It was a great shot.

"Against class conflict and materialism. For people, community, and idealistic living standards. I hand over Karl Marx and Kautsky to the fire," Goebbels continued, as the students dumped more books into the flames. "Against soul-fraying overestimation of the instinctual life. For the aristocracy of the human soul. I hand over the writings of Sigmund Freud to the fire."

v.

Paul stood at the open window, holding Meyer's letter in his hand. He could see the flames. He could also hear the speeches, since his radio was turned on.

A radio announcer was saying, in tones that were both excited and hushed, "*For those of you who are just now joining us, we're broadcasting live from the Berlin Opernplatz, where German students and university professors are holding a book-burning ceremony. Dr. Joseph Goebbels, Reich Minister for Public Enlightenment and Propaganda, is directing the proceedings. And here he is now, with more books to consign to the fire.*"

The radio announcer was still talking when Larissa Hoffmann came into the room.

"You know what a light sleeper your father is, Paul," she said. "Please turn off that radio."

When he didn't move, she went over to the radio and switched it off herself. A murmur of voices, which came from the nearby square, could still be heard in the room. The smoke had drifted in, too.

"If you don't care about your own health," she was saying as she went to the window and slammed it shut, closing the heavy curtains as well, "you should at least think of others. You know how sensitive I am to smoke. I can hardly breathe. Paul! Where are you going?"

vi.

He ran. He wanted to find a taxi, but all he could find were people and smoke. He turned a corner and the Opernplatz loomed up ahead of him. But it was not a scene he recognized. The Opernplatz, the square that faced the University of Berlin, was a place where books should be celebrated and revered, where ideas should be debated in an atmosphere of respect and sobriety. To light a bonfire there, of all places, was to turn out the lights of civilization and return the world to chaos.

Why didn't someone speak up, he wondered? Why didn't someone grab the microphone from that ridiculous man who was shouting and shaking his fist, and say, "Friends, this is not the way! Problems we have, differences there are, but once a destroying angel is unleashed in the world, who can restrain it? Let's demand a real community, real ideals. We are too good for this rhetoric of hate and demonization of others, too wise to believe that this path of silencing the voices of those with whom we disagree leads anywhere, except to our own destruction."

But no one stepped forward. Like him, everyone standing in the square on that spring night was mesmerized by the spectacle.

"That Goebbels knows how to throw the dogs a bone," he murmured, and then wondered where those words had come from.

Meanwhile, the German Propaganda Minister continued, "Against falsification of our history and disparagement of its great figures. For respect for our past. I hand over the writings of Emil Ludwig Kohn and Werner Hegemann to the fire."

Paul recognized a few faces standing on the podium, behind Goebbels. He didn't see Professor Hurst, but this really wasn't the old man's type of show. He was surprised, though, that Professor Laufer wasn't amongst the crowd of university officials standing on the stage.

A quick look behind him, where the bonfire was blazing away, solved the mystery. Laufer, dressed in his Brown Shirt uniform, was busy with the books and the students—not teaching the students, unless teaching them how to throw the books into the center of the bonfire qualified as education.

Paul came nearer to the fire and for a moment he caught the eye of his former thesis advisor. Laufer had plucked an old manuscript from the pile of books still waiting to be destroyed and he waved it in Paul's direction with a broad smile. It was the manuscript of *The Banished Heart*. Moments later it was ashes.

And still the Minister of Propaganda was speaking, his face ecstatically exultant as he reached the climax of his speech. "Out of these ashes the phoenix of a new age will arise. Oh, century! Oh, science! It is a joy to be alive!"

Somewhere in the crowd a group of students began to sing. The song spread, but Paul didn't wait for it to reach him. He darted down an alleyway, narrowly missing hurtling into some drunken Brown Shirts who were singing a song of their own.

A taxi came into view and he flagged it down.

vii.

It was already after midnight, but it might have been morning, if the size of the crowd swarming about the train station was any indication. Porters quickly pushed their carts loaded high with luggage to the tracks, while families and solitary travelers followed their belongings to the waiting trains.

"Watch where you're going!" one of the porters shouted to Paul, who had wandered into a cart's path and caused a suitcase to fall off.

He knew that Meyer must be in the crowd somewhere, with the others. But there were so many people, and so much noise. Above him the voice of the train announcer was shouting out the departure times and the places, so many places. Ahead of him a young child, who had apparently gotten separated from his parents, was wailing. "Mama! Mama!" the child cried out, helplessly. Paul stared at the child, stirred by the memory of ... something. But there was too much noise, too many people to think. The place fairly hummed with a heady mixture of tension and excitement and danger. Then a woman rushed in front of him and swooped up the crying boy in her arms and disappeared back into the crowd.

It was Meyer who spotted Paul, since Meyer was actually looking for Franz, who hadn't yet arrived. He called out to Paul, and soon they were standing off to the side of a departure gate, where it was a little quieter.

"I don't understand your letter," Paul said. "You're not an actor. Neither are Franz and Joseph."

"It was the best we could do on short notice. Sarah does part-time work for one of those Jewish cultural organizations, and a theatre company was scheduled to give performances in Palestine. She added our names to the list. Hopefully, the British immigration agents won't look at our forged papers too closely."

"They'll have to let us in," said Joseph, who had joined them, along with Sarah. "If they make a fuss, we'll recite that 'Quality of Mercy' speech by that Shakespeare of yours. And if that doesn't melt their hearts, we'll threaten to recite the complete works of Shakespeare, in German, until they let us in."

"Have you decided to come with us, Paul?" asked Sarah, who was looking terribly efficient and terribly worried, as usual. "I don't have papers for you, but maybe on the train we can ..."

Paul shook his head.

Once she saw that she didn't have to worry about yet another person, Sarah lost interest in Paul and nervously scanned the crowd for Franz, her missing thespian.

Meanwhile, Paul continued to question Meyer. "But what's the point? Surely you don't intend to stay in Palestine, so why go there?"

"I do intend to stay. We all do. Once we reach Haifa, we're going to disappear," said Meyer.

"Disappear?"

"There are Jews there who can give us new papers, so we can work. Meyer Aronstein will no longer exist. I'll be a new person."

"But what about your studies, your medical career? Your practice here, in Berlin?"

"It's over, Paul. Don't be the last one to see it."

"There he is! Franz! Over here!" Sarah called out.

Franz rushed over to them, his arms filled with packages.

"What happened to you?" Sarah demanded. "Why are you so late?"

"You try buying theatrical supplies when Goebbels is putting on a show," said Franz. "I hope what I bought is all right." He removed a tin of stage make-up from one of the bags. "Do actors really use this stuff?"

"Sometimes," said Sarah. "The main thing is that everyone has something in his suitcase, so that all of you look like you're actors, in case the border inspectors check. What else did you get?"

Franz pulled out a large red wig that had long and stringy hair. Joseph grabbed the wig and put it on his head and made a clownish face. "How do I look?"

"Take it off," said Paul.

"Why?" asked Joseph.

"That's a Judas wig."

"What's a Judas wig?" asked Franz.

"Actors used to wear one when they played a Jewish character. It's insulting."

"I can't believe you wasted our money on this, Franz," said Joseph, removing the wig from his head.

"How was I supposed to know? I'm not an actor."

They were interrupted by the announcement that their train was getting ready to depart.

"Here, Paul," said Joseph, tossing him the red wig. "We won't need this."

Joseph and Franz went with Sarah to the train.

"Come with us, Paul," said Meyer.

"Leave everything, now?"

"Sometimes that's the only way."

People were rushing past them, in a mad scramble to reach the train. It would be so easy to join the crowd, let himself be guided like a wave drifting toward the shore. But if he let go, if he was no longer Paul Hoffmann, who would he be?

"I can't go," he said.

"You still believe in Germany?"

"I have to believe in something."

The train let out a large burst of steam. Meyer turned and disappeared down the platform. Then the gate to the train tracks was closed.

Paul watched the cloud of steam grow. He heard the whistle blow, shrill and loud. Then the train lurched forward, accompanied by its clouds of glory, and began its slow departure from the station.

He stood watching it go, grasping with one hand the closed wrought iron gate and with the other the red wig, which he clutched to his heart.

"But ..."

A last billow of steam filled the air. There was no train. There was no Paul Hoffmann. There was no world. There was only a glimpse of red, and then it too was gone.

THE END

ABOUT THE AUTHOR

Libi Astaire is an award-winning author who often writes about Jewish history. She is also the author of the Ezra Melamed Mystery Series, a historical mystery series about Regency London's Jewish community, whose first volume, *The Disappearing Dowry*, was a Sydney Taylor Notable Book in 2010; *Terra Incognita*, a novel about Spanish villagers who discover they are descended from *Anusim*, Jews who were forced to convert to Christianity during the Middle Ages; and several volumes of Chassidic tales. She lives in Jerusalem, Israel. For updates about future books, visit her website at www.libiastaire.weebly.com.

Also by Libi Astaire

Terra Incognita
A Novel about the Crypto-Jews of Spain

Take a virtual trip to Catalonia with this story of a sleepy Catalan village that one day wakes up to discover a long-buried secret: the villagers are all descended from Anusim, Spanish Jews who were forced to convert to Christianity during the Middle Ages.

Terra Incognita tells the story of the Bonet family, residents of a tiny Catalan village called Sant Joan Januz. Vidal Bonet is a young businessman determined to revive his dying village by building a luxury resort. His grandfather, Miquel, is just as determined to keep the village locked away from strangers and their prying eyes.

Their battle for the future of Sant Joan Januz is further complicated by the arrival of a Jewish-American graduate student from Kansas, Chaim Green, who is sure the villagers are his long-lost relatives. And, finally, there is Clara Bonet, who has reluctantly taken on the role of the family's matriarch just when the village's long buried secret is accidentally uncovered.

Both poignant and funny, *Terra Incognita* is a journey of personal discovery that will resonate with anyone who has ever gone on a quest to discover their past - or who has ever lain awake at night wondering where in the world they are going.

PRAISE FOR
THE EZRA MELAMED MYSTERY SERIES

Jane Austen meets Sherlock Holmes when a crime wave sweeps through 19th-century London's Jewish community and the adventures of wealthy-widower-turned-sleuth Ezra Melamed are recorded for posterity by Miss Rebecca Lyon, a young lady not quite at the marriageable age.

The Disappearing Dowry
A 2010 Sydney Taylor Notable Book Award Winner

"A quick-paced, absorbing read." —*Jerusalem Post*

"One of the book's strengths as a work of historical fiction is that it moves beyond just "local color," weaving a plot that depends on events in British and Jewish history that may not be well-known to US readers, but which were integral to the experiences of early 19th century Jews." —Jewish Book Council

The Ruby Spy Ring

"Highly recommended." —Kaet's Weblog

"The voice of the narrator, Rebecca Lyon, a Jewish girl of about 16, has a fresh and sometimes hilariously innocent perspective that makes the book a lot of fun. This kind of period piece should never take itself too seriously and Libi has hit the right note in this book." —Maven Mall

Tempest in the Tea Room
"Nicely written and very entertaining." —Amazon.com

Made in the USA
Charleston, SC
25 March 2013